STEVE
THE
ZOMBIE

STEPHEN WAYNE

Typesetting by Istvan Szabo (Sapphire Guardian International, www.sapphireguardian.com)
Cover Design by Mirko Fermani

ISBN (Paperback): 978-615-01-8095-3
ISBN (Hardcover): 978-615-82317-0-1
ISBN (EPub): 978-615-82317-1-8
ISBN (Kindle): 978-615-82317-2-5

www.waynebooks.com

My head throbs, my vision fractures. My body is a silent battle-ground amidst a relentless storm of devastation. Each agonizing pulse of pain in my veins is a testament to the cells that the disease, like a ruthless executioner, mercilessly annihilates. Fever consumes me, centering on a mark on my neck. I am dying, yet I persist. The anguished cries of men and women, external manifestations of the internal torment I endure, reverberate through the air as death engulfs the world.

Initially, my sight blurred by shadows and distortions, slowly starts to sharpen, as though the world is materializing from a smoky murkiness. Forms meld from the darkness, growing more distinct and identifiable. As the mist in my perceptual field lifts, the environment around me begins to harden, assuming a more discernible, more palpable shape.

As clarity gradually returns to my sight, I become increasingly aware of the details around me - the subtle imperfections in the pavement, the reflected city lights glinting off pristine shop windows, and the graffiti-streaked walls that bear witness to the city's vibrant culture. The sun has retreated beyond the horizon, abandoning a soft twilight radiance that filters through the spaces between towering skyscrapers. The waning daylight casts a tranquil, yet disquieting ambiance as shadows elongate and intensify along the street, succumbing to the encroaching darkness.

Moving with unexpected swiftness, I pass by lifeless bodies strewn in pools of blood on the street. Yet, my mind remains too numb to fully grasp the unfolding horror before my eyes. I find myself amid a mass of people, rushing alongside them as if we're all seeking escape from the terror that has seized the city. The gut-wrenching screams of victims are magnified, resonating through the streets and amplifying the pervasive sense of impending doom that saturates the air.

The sight of the fallen triggers an indistinct sense of urgency within me. A persistent pulse deep within my consciousness hints at a desperate need to protect someone, to reach someone. Yet, the specifics remain frustratingly out of grasp, like attempting to catch smoke with my bare hands. The person's identity is shrouded in a dense fog of uncertainty, stirring profound feelings of loss and frustration. Who was it that I wanted to protect, and from what, and why? Faces, names, voices – they all coalesce into an indistinct blur, lost amidst the swirling tempest of my thoughts.

A deep, menacing growl sends an involuntary shudder through me. The sound is terrifying, and I instinctively seek its source, fearing a monstrous predator lurks nearby. Attempting to turn my head, I find my movement restricted; I can only shift my eyes. As I scrutinize my surroundings, my muscles tense in apprehension. Gradually, I notice the disconcerting peculiarity of the individuals around me. Their movements are jerky and uncoordinated, their eyes are bloodshot, devoid of humanity, and their irises emit an eerie orange glow. It's at this chilling moment I realize I am encircled by zombies, their guttural growls reflecting my own. The horrifying truth strikes me - I'm one of them.

I am trapped within my own body, desperate to scream, to cry out, but my voice has betrayed me, producing only inhuman, guttural groans. The world appears different; colors are muted, sounds are more grating, and the iron-rich scent of blood is an assault on my senses. My stomach churns in disgust, but concurrently, an unfamiliar and abhorrent hunger stirs. An unspeakable craving claws its way from the depths of my gut, intensifying as an incessant itch pervades my flesh. It feels as though a million tiny insects burrow beneath my skin, fostering a horrific urge to rip and tear at human flesh. This ravenous beast within yearns for satisfaction with a meal I find morally repugnant, a perverse desire that permeates my thoughts, compelling me towards unimaginable atrocities.

Amid this sensory onslaught, an unyielding inferno of pain sears through me. Every fiber of my being warps in an agonizing dance of metamorphosis. My skin grotesquely distorts, my bones ache with an intensity bordering on madness, and my muscles convulse in an unwilling ballet of adaptation — a cruel display of my transformation from man to beast. Amid this torment, cursed blood courses through my veins like ice, radiating a bitter chill from my fingertips to my core, marking my gradual descent into inhumanity.

The pain recedes, replaced by an equally disconcerting numbness. Drawing a ritual breath into lungs that no longer require it, each hesitant heartbeat renders my body feeling more alien, more disconnected. My beastly form moves of its own accord, like a marionette controlled by unseen strings, hunting and stalking with a predatory instinct I never knew I possessed. My muscles twitch and convulse, each movement beyond my control, a macabre dance dictated by a sinister puppeteer who has relegated my consciousness to the backseat.

Now, I am part of the horde, an appalling spectacle amidst lifeless humans and terrifying creatures flooding the streets. We are zombies, an unstoppable tide of reanimated beings. Yet even as my physical form succumbs to this horrifying transformation, remnants of my humanity cling stubbornly to my consciousness, refusing to be entirely consumed. Despite everything, an echo of my humanity persists, a spectral presence within the monster I've become.

We approach a luxurious restaurant with a bustling terrace, our pace somewhere between a walk and a run. Patrons sit at elegantly set tables, engaging in lively conversation and laughter, utterly oblivious to the nightmare that's about to unfold. The contrast between the carefree atmosphere on the terrace and the gruesome reality beyond its borders is striking.

Without warning, the swarm bursts forth, closing the gap between the unsuspecting diners and the ravenous zombies in mere seconds. Despite our speed and the apparent onset of the outbreak, we seem to catch the people by surprise, as if they have no idea of the horror that's unfolding.

The undead lunge at the diners, their feral snarls filling the air. The guests' laughter turns to screams of terror as they frantically attempt to escape the clutches of their grotesque assailants. Elegant glassware and fine china crash to the ground, shattering into pieces as the tables are overturned in the chaos. Panic-stricken individuals scramble to find shelter, some desperately climbing over the terrace railing in a futile attempt to flee the cruel onslaught.

The pounding of living hearts echoes in my ears, their terror mirroring in their eyes. Some are bitten, others consumed—to my surprise, the transformation from human to zombie occurs in mere seconds post-bite. Reason eludes my numbed mind amidst this horrifying spectacle. Each face I encounter is no longer discerned as a friend, a neighbor, or a stranger, but seen as a potential feast, an answer to an insatiable hunger unfamiliar to me.

Amid this ghastly parade, I make a startling realization. Unlike the others in the horde, my body abstains from attacking or biting. It feels as though my consciousness and the infection are locked in a fierce internal battle for control. Yet, the monstrous hunger within me seethes, straining like a chained beast yearning to partake in the mindless violence. I am trapped in a tug-of-war between the insatiable feeding urge and the vestiges of my human nature. My captive conscience watches in horror as the primal impulses of my grotesque form escalate. I wage war against this monstrous instinct, each moment a desperate struggle to retain any fragments of my humanity. These shards of my human self cling on tenaciously, flickering like a candle in the face of a relentless storm.

The formerly peaceful terrace is now a horrifying display of carnage and despair, a stark reminder of the nightmarish reality engulfing the city. The sounds of sirens and screams reverberate in the distance, vividly illustrating the chaos and desperation occurring elsewhere.

As the swarm of the undead horrifically feasts on its victims, tearing flesh and splattering blood, I begin to scrutinize the other zombies more closely. My consciousness attempts to discern who these horrific creatures might have been before their existence was consumed by this nightmarish state. Among the macabre forms, a few stand out.

One, wearing a fast-food uniform with a tag bearing the name 'Sally', barely visible beneath layers of blood and grime. Another, garbed in an oil-stained mechanic's uniform, sports a nametag that reads 'Bob'. His hands, once skilled at manipulating delicate machinery, are now clenched into stiff, unyielding fists. A bus driver, unrecognizable from the diligent figure he once was, now keeps pace with the horde, his vacant stare belying his previous attentiveness. A once-fragile elderly woman follows suit, gripping a gardening tool, her twisted, contorted frame and demented orange eyes devoid of the wisdom they once held. Lastly, a jogger staggers along, clad in athletic gear. His ArcticAde soda bottle, still strapped to his wrist, serves as a cruel reminder of his former dedication to fitness, now a glaring irony in his current state.

The rest, men and women alike, are indistinguishable, their clothing and features providing no insight into who they might have been. Their identities are erased, swallowed by the relentless tide of the infection, leaving behind only these monstrous shells.

Moving past the restaurant's frontage, our monstrous likenesses are cast back from the gleaming window panes, bathed in the spectral glow of the streetlights. My own reflection catches my attention—a grotesque mirror image that's both familiar and terrifying. My hair, once neatly combed, now hangs disheveled over my forehead. My eyes, normally warm and welcoming, burn with a haunting orange glow, devoid of any human warmth. My skin, once the healthy shade of an outdoors enthusiast, is now pallid and lifeless, contrasting starkly against my neatly tailored suit. The creature that stares back at me from the glass is an entity spun from nightmares. It borrows my features, my attire, but it isn't me. Not anymore.

The sight of our lumbering group, hauntingly trailing in my wake, is chilling. Among them is a young basketball player, his once-vibrant jersey now ripped and stained; a man exuding an academic air, perhaps a teacher in his previous life, his glasses skewed and shattered; and a construction worker, his hard hat still clinging stubbornly to his head, a poignant reminder of his former life. The faces of these erstwhile ordinary men and women are now defaced by the ghastly features of their undead state, their unique identities obliterated under the relentless hunger driving them forward.

I can't help but notice that some among us, including the jogger, bear no visible bite marks. Their skin, though pallid and marred, seems untouched by the gnashing teeth of the horde. This disturbing realization implies that these individuals must have been contaminated prior to any physical attack. This chilling revelation suggests that the virus had been spreading through more insidious, unseen methods, broadening its scope beyond the domain of the overtly violent. The true extent of the contagion appears more ominous, as the unseen paths of this plague reveal themselves within the ranks of the horde.

Distant thumping of loud music grows steadily louder, guiding us towards our next destination. We soon arrive at the entrance of a luxurious club, where an eclectic mix of people, including pimps, ladies in extravagant attire, and other partygoers, wait in anticipation for their night of revelry to begin. The vibrant atmosphere stands in stark contrast to the terror lurking just beyond their awareness. As we draw closer, the chatter and laughter of the crowd is gradually replaced by a growing sense of unease. Confused glances are exchanged as they begin to register the monstrous grunts and heavy footsteps of the advancing swarm.

Suddenly, the rumble of a powerful engine cuts through the night's eerie silence. A sleek luxury sports car, its cobalt blue paint gleaming under the streetlights, roars to a stop in front of the club. Its design, a perfect blend of muscle and grace, commands the attention of everyone in the vicinity. The thunderous purr of the engine, harmonizing with the car's captivating aesthetics, draws in the gaze of everyone nearby. The crowd outside the club, previously engaged in chatter and laughter, now turns their attention to the dazzling spectacle before them. Even those who had caught a glimpse of the approaching undead, their faces marked with the initial signs of fear, find themselves momentarily distracted by the arrival of this luxurious chariot.

The driver's side door swings open, and a man steps out. Dressed in designer clothes that scream wealth and status, he radiates an aura of self-importance that's impossible to ignore. His face is familiar; a local nobody who shot to stardom overnight, all because he flashed his smile on television. His name, however, escapes me.

As he stands by his car, basking in the attention from the onlookers and their flashing cameras, his smug smile slowly fades. His eyes widen as he finally takes notice of the approaching horde, the grim reality of his situation dawning upon him. Panic seizes him and he stumbles back towards his car, desperate to escape the impending onslaught. He pushes the accelerator to the floor, hoping the powerful engine can outpace the encroaching chaos.

However, fate has other plans, as a bus careens into the car's side at the nearest intersection, turning the once-pristine vehicle into a mangled mess of metal and glass. The bus comes to a halt, and the bus driver, terrified by the accident he just participated in, stumbles out of the vehicle. The passengers, seemingly unharmed, start to emerge as well, their faces reflecting a mixture of shock and confusion.

The resounding crash captures the focus of the partygoers, diverting their attention from the steady encroachment of the undead. Instead of rushing to help the unfortunate driver, they whip out their phones and start filming the wreckage. Some of them call out mocking insults to the driver, with one yelling, "Hey, loser! Bet you wish you'd stayed home tonight, huh?"

Their lack of empathy and compassion is astounding, but it doesn't last long as the zombies close in on them with a sudden burst of speed from behind. The focus of the crowd shifts from the accident to the very real danger that now surrounds them.

The once-orderly line devolves into chaos, as partygoers scream and scatter in a desperate attempt to escape the ravenous monsters. Some of the zombies break off from the main group, targeting the passengers trying to flee the wreckage of the bus with little success. The club's booming music now serves as a chilling soundtrack to the carnage unfolding before its doors.

As the zombies relentlessly tear into their victims, the dropped phones of the now-doomed onlookers record the gruesome scene.

Some individuals manage to break free from the panicked crowd and flee into the night, their high heels and polished shoes pounding the pavement in a frenzied sprint for survival. Others are not so lucky, as the zombies close in, ripping and tearing at their once-glamorous attire, their flesh, and their lives. The opulent entrance of the club, once a symbol of carefree indulgence, has become a nightmarish scene of death and destruction.

Witnessing this heartbreaking spectacle, the lingering sparks of my humanity persist; they serve as a constant reminder of the life I once led. The vestiges of my human self hold tight to my awareness, refusing to be fully extinguished. Amidst the chaos and gore, I am a mere observer, powerless to control the beast I have become.

My mind is a disarray of fragmented memories, obscured by the foggy veil of my condition. However, amongst the chaos, a familiar face flickers within the murkiness, asserting its presence. A woman - her eyes brimming with a complex cocktail of love and fear, her lips whispering words long since forgotten. The more I try to reach into the depths of my mind, the clearer the image becomes. She was... she was my girlfriend.

Her name eludes me, like a melody I can't quite recall. But then, a heated argument from our past rises from the depths of my memories, cutting through the silence and chaos that engulfs me. A plea, resonating with frustration and desperation, echoes in my mind, "Why can't you just listen to me for once?!" Her voice, even in memory, is filled with raw emotion - a blend of anger, fear, and something else... love? It bounces off the walls of my decaying mind, each word hitting like a physical blow. The emotional gravity of the moment forces me to a standstill as the memory washes over me.

Her name... It teeters on the edge of my consciousness, like a word on the tip of the tongue. Suddenly, it clicks into place. Sarah. Her name was Sarah. The revelation sends a rush of emotion through me, like a crashing wave, stirring up a storm of regret, loss, and a strange, lingering affection. I can almost see her, standing defiantly before me, her expressive eyes alight with passion. The fragrance of her perfume engulfs my senses as the memory surfaces, an alluring combination of sweet, floral elements with hints of iris, earthy subtleties, and deliciously tempting gourmand touches. This aroma, so intimately tied to her, evokes feelings of warmth, happiness, and comfort, recalling shared moments of closeness.

Sarah... How could I have forgotten her? Upon visualizing her face in my mind, an insistent urgency returns, resurrecting the desperate need to protect her from the encroaching nightmare. But did I save her? I'm consumed by the uncertainty. My sacrifice, I hope, was not in vain. The memory of a searing, unbearable pain breaks through, serving as a chilling reminder of the moment my fate was sealed by the merciless bite that condemned me.

My body relentlessly marches on, propelled by an insatiable hunger gnawing at my core. I'm trapped within this monstrous shell, a grotesque parody of my former self, condemned to witness the horrors it yearns to commit in my name. The world I once knew contorts under this monstrous existence; familiar landmarks distort into alien terrains, people transform into ambulatory feasts, and the city's comforting rhythm gives way to a dissonant cacophony of chaos. This waking nightmare represents a reality that is both mine and yet disturbingly alien.

But as I gaze upon the landscape, somehow I recognize the cobbled streets, the brickwork, the haunting shadows cast by lamplight - all elements deeply etched in the corners of my murky memory. The familiar structures, the grocery store where I once shopped, the tidy little restaurant where Sarah and I would occasionally dine, the glossy shop windows showcasing their prime merchandise, each sparks fleeting glimpses of a life I once lived. This place was my sanctuary, where I experienced joy, shared warmth, and nurtured relationships. Now, it serves as the grim stage for my nightmarish reality. The remnants of my past life intertwine with the uncanny silence blanketing these streets, creating an unsettling calm before an inevitable storm.

At a nearby intersection, a patrol car rushes across, its siren wailing and the eerie glow of its red and blue lights slicing through the dim streetlights. The sight of it, passing in front of the horde at a distance, triggers an unexpected spark of recognition within me. It nudges a dormant memory—this was the beat of Murphy and Brown, two officers with whom I worked on an unsolved murder case.

Suddenly, I find myself standing at a past crime scene with Murphy and Brown, their faces blurry in the periphery of my recollections. The alternating glow of red and blue lights paint our surroundings in an otherworldly hue as we stand near their patrol car. As I duck under the yellow "Do Not Cross" tape, I flash my badge, its metallic surface glinting in the eerie light, and introduce myself to the pair of officers, "Detective Steve...". My voice trails off as my family name fades from memory, just as elusive as the fleeting tranquility of the past.

My name was Steve, that much comes back to me. Though my first name resurfaces, the rest remains shrouded in the fog of my fragmented memories. I had been a detective in this district, that much is clear. I found myself at the heart of investigating the bizarre events that had draped the city in a veil of mystery and terror. I remember people attacking each other with brutal ferocity, biting and tearing at one another like crazed animals. Yet my memory stumbles, leaving the specifics of my investigation just out of reach.

Suddenly, amid the savage snarls and relentless march of the horde, a bout of laughter pierces through, jolting me from my grim introspection. The mass descends upon a group of young people who, at first, laugh and mock the approaching zombies. "Yo, look at these guys!" one of them jeers, "Another one believes the zombie apocalypse is here, huh?" They continue to chuckle, still blissfully unaware of the situation.

But the air thickens with the acrid scent of fear as the reality sets in and the zombies attack. The young people's terror-stricken faces are etched with the horror of the nightmarish reality that has befallen them. Their desperate screams echo hauntingly through the desolate streets as some are devoured alive.

Others, overtaken by overwhelming fear, try to escape from the unyielding pursuit of the monstrous beings that may have once been their friends or neighbors. "Get outta here, dude! This ain't no prank! They're the real deal!" a voice, trembling with dread, rings out, abruptly dispelling the naive sense of security they had briefly enjoyed.

A young skateboarder narrowly escapes the initial onslaught, making his way to an intersection. He glances back, smirks, and shouts, "Ha! Can't catch me, losers!", convinced he's evaded his doom. His relief is short-lived as a zombie springs at him from a side street and he is devoured alive.

The horde then zeroes in on a young woman, no more than twenty. She attempts to flee, crying, "Someone, please help me!" She's wearing headphones, the music blaring loud enough to reach my ears even from within the horde. The dim streetlights cast a glow on her shirt, which bears a bold slogan: "Equal rights for zombies." This sight triggers a memory.

I recall a crowd of protesters donning similar shirts outside my precinct. They were self-proclaimed Social Justice Warriors aggressively demonstrating after an officer was forced to subdue a mentally disordered individual behaving aggressively, akin to a zombie. In a misguided attempt to etch their ideals into the minds of ordinary citizens, they ironically referred to the afflicted as zombies and the undead. Little did they know just how eerily accurate their jest would turn out to be.

Her obliviousness and absurd protest resonate with me. In my former life, I often pondered the insularity and naivety of such people, those comfortably cocooned, oblivious to the world beyond their limited scope. They rallied against moral ambiguity, seeking significance or notoriety. Many advocated for the most obscure causes, even journeying to quarries to speak up for distant arctic whales, as if their actions could genuinely affect these far-flung creatures.

Now, as her run slows to a desperate crawl, I see hopelessness etched in her eyes as the horde catches up. Her aspirations of being a savior are extinguished, reflecting her inability to save even herself. Her screams are swallowed by the encroaching darkness, drowned out by the chaos and insatiable hunger propelling us forward. Despite the grim scenario, an unexpected wave of sympathy for her swells within me as she rises from the black asphalt, joining us in wreaking havoc on the world she once sought to save.

Watching her, my detective instincts surge, demanding justice for her and all the other victims, myself included. Restless, my mind yearns to unravel the mystery of this terrifying contagion, to revisit the evidence I've collected and the statements I took ever since this case was assigned to me. But the infection overwhelms me, like the fatigue of sleeplessness that eventually forces one to surrender to slumber, it begins to blur my vision. My body, commandeered by the beast that the virus has made of me, continues its rampage. Yet, my mind clings to the hope that the solution to this nightmare is hidden within the fragments of my past.

Gradually, my fever dream takes over, swallowing me into its depths. I find myself adrift in a sea of disjointed thoughts and experiences. The world around me becomes distorted, and haunting images from my past meld with the nightmarish present. Colors swirl and bleed together, the tumult of sounds fades, and the very fabric of reality begins to unravel.

As the horde strides on, my consciousness distances from the real events unfolding around me. Instead, fragments of my memory overtake my awareness, coalescing into a surreal fever dream that feels all too real. It's as if the world is made of ink, lacking any true details or depth. Although these events have happened before, they hold fresh, crucial clues to the nightmare I'm currently living.

In this dreamlike state, I'm compelled to investigate, seeking to uncover the hidden truths buried beneath the monochromatic haze. The boundaries between reality and imagination blur, weaving a bizarre tapestry that leaves me navigating an uncertain path through the shadows of my past.

I find myself sitting in my detective car, the door wide open, as the vehicle seems to meld with my office and desk – two places where I spent most of my career. Slow rain falls from above, defying gravity, while the darkness of the night is pierced by the light on my desk.

I sip a cup of coffee, and the radio crackles to life, saying, "Detective, we've got a Code 10-54 at 457 Oakwood Avenue. Possible drug-related incident. We need you on the scene immediately." Holding the coffee pouring jar, I respond, "Copy that.

I'm on my way." I pour myself another cup of coffee and drink it before closing the car door and turning the ignition.

Setting down the empty cup on my desk, I look up to find myself parked outside a suspect's house. The sudden transition between spaces leaves me momentarily disoriented. As I exit the car, two police officers approach me, their strides oddly reversed, as if reality's laws have been defied. Their features blur into the surreal surroundings, adding to the eerie ambiance of this dreamscape. As they turn to address me, one of them begins detailing the grim events that led us here.

"Detective, we were dispatched to this house, home of Jian Li and his family. Li inexplicably massacred his wife, Mei, and their two children, Xue and Jia. Upon our arrival, Li attacked us like a rabid beast," he recounts.

Their names resurface in my mind - Officers Davis and Ramirez - yet their faces remain indistinct throughout our exchange, failing to solidify into any recognizable form.

"It was unlike anything we've ever encountered," Officer Davis continues. "Li showed no reaction to pain and demonstrated uncanny strength. We eventually subdued him only after shooting him multiple times."

Officer Ramirez motions for me to follow him. With my first step, I am instantaneously inside the house, immersed in the horrific aftermath of the massacre. The walls seem to bleed; the floor undulates beneath my feet, almost as if it were a sentient entity repulsed by the atrocities it witnessed.

The sheer brutality of the carnage is overwhelming. Li's family has been torn apart, their lifeless bodies sprawled across the room, bearing the unmistakable marks of a frenzied attack. The colors in the room are both vivid and muted, as if reality is shifting between the starkness of the tragedy and the dreamlike haze that envelops it.

My instincts tell me that this is no ordinary case of drug-induced violence; there is something far more sinister at play. The air around me feels heavy with a foreboding sense of dread, and the shadows seem to dance and twist into unsettling shapes, echoing the chaos that had unfolded in this once-happy home.

As I try to make sense of the dreamlike scene before me, I find myself struggling to separate fact from the feverish distortions of my dream state. The boundaries between the two blur, leaving me to navigate a landscape that is both terrifyingly real and hauntingly ethereal.

The faceless Ramirez approaches me, his form shifting and indistinct, as if he is struggling to maintain his presence in this phantasmagoric landscape. "I've never seen anything like this before, detective," he says, his voice echoing strangely. The walls seem to absorb his words, rippling with the emotions they carry. "We pumped five bullets into him, and it barely slowed him down. It's like something was fueling him, pushing him to keep going despite the injuries."

As Ramirez speaks, I notice the shadows flickering around him, creating unsettling patterns that draw my gaze. He hesitates for a moment, then adds, "And there was this weird thing with his eyes. Their irises were glowing orange. At first, I thought it was some strange play of lights and shadows, but I couldn't shake the feeling that it was something more."

The officer's words only serve to solidify my suspicions that we are dealing with something far beyond the scope of our previous experiences. As I examine the perpetrator's body, I notice a sixth bullet wound, a clean shot through his head. It is this final bullet that had ultimately stopped him, but not before he had left a trail of devastation in his wake.

From the head wound, something small and wriggling emerges. It transforms before my eyes into a colorful butterfly, fluttering its wings as it takes flight. I can't help but wonder if the butterfly symbolizes the perpetrator's transformation, a chilling reminder that whatever had driven this man to commit such heinous acts was unlike anything we had ever encountered before.

The very fabric of reality seems to be unraveling around us, blurring the lines between the waking world and the fevered nightmare that has gripped me. I examine the scene meticulously, my surroundings warped and dreamlike as I search for clues that could shed light on the cause of the man's baffling metamorphosis.

Among the scattered remnants of a once-ordinary life, I find various seemingly inconsequential details: a receipt from a recent grocery run filled with vegetables and healthy items, stretching and twisting like a ribbon in the wind; a stack of unopened bills that pulse with an eerie glow; fitness magazines and self-help books that meld and morph as I try to read their titles; a yoga mat coiled like a snake, ready to strike.

In the refrigerator, I find a seemingly endless line of VitalVibe fitness drinks, ArcticAde soda cans, and RefreshFizz healthy sodas, as if peering into the back of a truck. All these clues point to a man who was health-conscious and focused on maintaining his vitality. Yet, despite these efforts, he had not been under the influence of any known drugs or substances. Instead, these seemingly unrelated clues point towards a more sinister explanation – that he had fallen prey to a new, enigmatic virus, or perhaps experienced the side effects of a vaccine, both of which had invaded his mind and body, transforming him into a monstrous killer.

As I glance into other rooms, my memory merges some of them together, creating an uncanny blend of spaces. The living room bleeds into the kitchen, the kitchen sink morphing into a bathtub filled with dishes, and a bedroom with a bed made of sofa cushions. The washing machines, three of them standing side by side in the bedroom, churn loudly in unison, their discordant hum filling the air with an unsettling resonance. As I continue to examine the scene, I notice the washing machines' windows not only churning clothes but also displaying the local news about this very event, as if they have merged with a TV. The surrealism of the dream persists as I watch the news, which also shows a blurred version of me, the detective assigned to the case.

I approach the washing machines and use a TV remote to crank down their volume so I can hear the news more clearly. The reporter on the screen addresses me directly, asking, "Detective, can you provide any insights into this case?"

I respond, aware of the bizarre situation but unfazed in the dream, "At this point, we're just beginning our investigation, and it's too early to draw any conclusions or make any comments."

The reporter nods, and the washing machines continue to display the news as I resume my search for clues, trying to make sense of this nightmarish scene and understand the sinister force that had transformed an ordinary man into a horrific killer.

As I step into another room, my surroundings shift dramatically and oddly, the ground beneath me undulating like waves as

I find myself under a bridge at a different crime scene. Though the change in location is abrupt, it doesn't seem to bother me. Here, the air is heavy with a fog that swirls around me, distorting the scene like an impressionist painting. Another perpetrator lies dead, his head blown apart by a shotgun blast, the last resort by the police to stop him. This man, a homeless individual, had massacred a group of fellow homeless people, their bodies now covered by body bags nearby that appear to pulse and breathe in the dream's twisted reality.

Officer Martinez stands beside me in the dream, her image sharply defined against the foggy landscape of my subconscious. Her green eyes glow, the high cheekbones adding definition to her radiant face. Her voice, heavy with burden, echoes in the misty silence, "Steve, I've never seen anything like this. He was more beast than man. The rage, the violence... It was inhuman. I had no choice. I had to shoot him. Please understand."

"I believe you, Rosa. I believe you," I reassure her, drawing her into an embrace to soothe her frayed nerves. Her face, full of emotion, is as clear in my memory as it is in the dream. The faces of other colleagues fade into obscurity, but hers remains distinct. The question lingers – why?

As the dreamscape morphs and swirls around us, faceless people gather, their voices melding into a chorus of activist slogans. "Equal rights for zombies!" one of them cries out, and others follow with shouts of, "Zombie lives matter!", "Don't discriminate against the undead!", "Justice for the sufferers!", and "Equal treatment for the infected!" They raise their voices in a discordant symphony, their passion misguided, their cause misunderstood.

As we hold each other, Rosa begins to transform, her once soft form taking on the stillness of a statue. Suddenly, she crumbles, disintegrating into a cold, unyielding dust. From the dust, a mesmerizing swarm of bright blue butterflies emerges, flickering and dancing around me like ephemeral fireflies. Their ethereal glow bathes me in an otherworldly light, casting shifting shadows across my face. As I watch, entranced, the glow of the butterflies begins to dim, their vibrant blue hues slowly fading away. Along with them, the protest around us seems to dissolve, leaving me standing alone in an abrupt silence.

The scene shifts, transporting me back to the crime scene under the bridge, where the grisly details effortlessly intertwine with the phantasmagoric landscape of my dream. Amidst the contorted bodies and the torn remains of the homeless encampment, I discover various seemingly insignificant details that offer glimpses into the lives these individuals led.

Scraps of discarded food create a mosaic of vibrant colors on the ground, as if painted by a master artist. The collection of mismatched clothes, blankets, and other items form an otherworldly landscape that defies logic. There are piles of soda cans collected from the streets and gathered like treasures, scattered and overflowing like a cascading waterfall. They seem to shimmer and shift colors as if they were alive, the brand names changing with each blink. In another corner, I find a pile of discarded grocery bags that appear to breathe, each exhale emitting a soft rustle, as if they were filled with a hidden life force. Among the debris, I spot a cluster of fruit and vegetable scraps that shift and morph, blurring the lines between organic and inorganic matter.

As my mind races to make connections, observing these strange and surreal elements, I strive to find a thread that might link these details and help me understand the monstrous transformations that had taken place. I can't shake the feeling that these seemingly unrelated clues hold the key to uncovering the dark force driving ordinary people to commit such heinous acts of violence.

As I continue to search for clues, the fever dream morphs once again. The world around me dissolves into a whirlwind of color and darkness, and I find myself in the coroner's room. The room has merged with a shooting range, creating a bizarre and unsettling environment. The coroner, Dr. Granger, his face now clear in my mind's eye, sits with me in front of a table piled with more than twenty corpses, their lifeless forms twisted and contorted. The lines on his face and the graying hair at his temples suggest years of experience in his field. We eat Chinese food as the corpses burn like a campfire, casting eerie shadows on the walls.

Behind us, in one of the lanes at the shooting range, a veteran SWAT officer named Jackson practices his aim by firing at zombie targets with his pistol. His muscular frame and determined expression speak to his years of service, and his steely eyes seem to never waver. I remember both the coroner's and Jackson's faces, perhaps because we have worked together extensively in the past.

The doctor, between bites of food, speaks to me about the killers. "These perpetrators were a diverse and terrifying group, Steve. Their minds were consumed by an aggressive and virulent infection that had obliterated their sanity. They hailed from all walks of life: the wealthy, the middle class, the impoverished, and even the homeless. Most of them had no history of drug or substance use, complicating our efforts to identify any commonalities among the infected."

The dead bodies inside the freezers begin to knock, as if protesting the progress of our investigation. The coroner barks at them, "Quiet down in there! We're already working on your case!" They fall silent.

I turn to the doctor and say, "Despite the countless cases I've investigated, the connections between these perpetrators remain elusive, Doc. The seemingly random nature of their violent outbursts has left me drowning in a sea of dead ends and false leads. I've been searching for patterns and connections between the afflicted, but despite my efforts, I've found nothing. Jackson, what do you think?" I ask, glancing at the veteran SWAT officer.

"Feels like an impending zombie apocalypse, doesn't it?" Jackson's chuckle is hollow, a bleak humor ringing amidst the gunfire. He reloads his pistol, firing more rounds at the targets. "These things are on another level. Standard pistol rounds don't seem to bother them. We've had to resort to headshots," he demonstrates with a precision shot to a target's head. "Porello tried tasering one. It only bought us a few precious seconds before it lunged at us again."

"What do you suggest?" the Doc inquires, spitting into the campfire of bodies.

"We need to rethink our strategy. We might learn something from Martinez's ordeal," Jackson offers.

"She's on suspension because of that incident," I say, setting aside my Chinese food. "But honestly, I believe Rosa had no other choice. She wouldn't break protocol unless absolutely necessary."

Jackson, taken aback, questions, "How can you be so sure?"

"When Rosa first graduated from the academy, I supervised her probation," I explain.

Jackson lowers his pistol, turning his gaze towards me. Surprise and interest gleam in his eyes. "I didn't realize you two were that close."

I sigh, letting the flood of memories wash over me. "We were more than just colleagues. After her probation, Rosa and I remained partners on the beat for nearly two years, until my promotion to detective. We faced the daily grind together, celebrated small triumphs, learned hard lessons. Over time, Rosa — 'Flutter' as I used to call her — transformed from a rookie into a reliable ally and a trusted friend. She even managed to win over Sarah, something few of my female colleagues could do."

Jackson's expression changes, realization dawning as he understands the depth of my association with Martinez. At the same time, I grasp why Rosa, of all people, stands out so starkly in my dreams.

"The media will crucify her for doing what was right," Jackson mutters, quickly reloading his pistol and firing a few more rounds at another zombie target. "We're grappling with a threat that defies traditional strategies and comprehension. We must adjust our tactics, regardless of whether all the politicians, lawyers, activists and vocal NGOs, who are protecting the rights of the perpetrators and standing against the police, approve, or else we'll be overwhelmed."

The lights in the room start to flicker in a rhythmic pattern, bathing the area in a pulsating red and blue hue. Another officer,

Mitchell, with a face that seems somewhat blurred, enters the room and takes a seat with a heavy sigh. "Detective, we've got another one," he announces somberly.

"Steve. Bring him in," the Doc responds with a mixture of resignation and determination. "Let's see what we're dealing with this time."

I clink my beer bottle with the Doc's and share the story of the latest corpse. "You know, this one was taken down by a civilian, Mr. Donovan," I say as I pull a lever on the wall, causing another body to tumble onto the pile of burning corpses.

"Really?" the Doc asks, raising an eyebrow.

"Yeah, it's quite a tale," I respond. "The man was acting like a wild beast, attacking locals like a rabid animal. Mr. Donovan, who lived nearby, caught sight of the commotion from his backyard. He owns an impressive arsenal in his barn that would put a military base to shame."

The Doc leans in, clearly intrigued. "And what did he do?"

"Initially, Donovan tried to defuse the situation. He grabbed one of his rifles for protection and confronted the man, attempting to calm him down. But when the man jumped at him, Donovan had no choice but to protect himself," I explain. "With a single, precise shot, he neutralized the threat. It's not every day you see a civilian handle a crisis like this," I admit, my voice tinged with a mix of admiration and concern.

"I detect a hint of reservation," the Doc observes.

"It's a complex issue, Doc," I confess. "I'm generally wary of civilians possessing firearms. I've seen too many tragedies stem from misuse. Too many people aren't mentally equipped to handle firearms responsibly. Heck, some can't even handle a plastic butter knife without causing trouble. But this time…" I sigh, "Mr. Donovan was an exception. He was the right man in the right place at the right moment. Even so, the damage had been done. Eight people, including two kids, ended up in the hospital with deep cuts and scratches. The perpetrator, who behaved like a man on potent drugs, attacked with heightened strength. The first victim, a trained kickboxer named Mr. Taylor, defended himself with some well-timed punches and a spinning kick, knocking out the attacker's false teeth after his first bite missed. But even he was overwhelmed by the sheer force of the aggressor. After that, the man didn't stop; toothless, he turned to mauling. The confrontation left Mr. Taylor injured and forced him to withdraw, leaving the others exposed to the horrifying spectacle." I give a grim nod toward the burning corpse, a silent testament to the night's horrors. "I can't blame Mr. Donovan for shooting him."

The Doc muses, "Times like these bring out the best and worst in people. It's comforting to know there are still individuals willing to stand up and protect their community."

I nod, but my expression hardens. "The tragic irony is that now, Mr. Donovan, Mr. Taylor—and even Rosa—are being hounded by the Mayor, NGOs, and the media. They want to penalize them for doing what was necessary," I say, bitterness creeping into my voice.

"To hell with all of them." The familiar voice resonates from behind me, its stern and defiant tone instantly silencing the room. Surprised, I swivel around in my chair, suddenly finding myself in an entirely different setting. No longer am I in the sterile confines of a morgue but in the cozy, dim-lit interior of a bar at night.

Across from me, Rosa sits nonchalantly dressed in civilian clothes. Her gaze, steely and unwavering, takes me in. Other patrons inhabit the space around us, their faces blurred, identities insignificant in the grand scheme of our exchange. Yet, our quiet congregation is not unobserved. Beyond the bar's glass panes, wolves lurk, their sinister silhouettes punctuated by moonlight. Their predatory eyes are firmly locked onto Rosa, their growls a low, ominous hum breaking the silence of the night, underscoring their intent - they're on a hunt.

"When trouble lands on your doorstep," Rosa asserts, her voice slicing through the distorted strains of a familiar song playing in the background of the bar, "you can't always wait for someone else to come to the rescue. Especially not those who preach anti-weapon sentiments from the safety of their guarded houses. Sometimes, you have to be your own savior or the wolves will come and get you." Her gaze drifts momentarily towards the window, meeting the menacing stare of the prowling beasts, unflinching in the face of their silent threat.

Rosa's fingers tremble as she pulls a worn badge from her pocket. She studies it for a moment, lost in thought, then pushes it across the table towards me. Her face crumples, and her words come out in a choked whisper. "It's a messed-up world when the people defending themselves and others are the ones who end up being persecuted."

"I couldn't agree more," a voice murmurs from behind me. Startled, I whirl around to find the Doc, seated back in the morgue, a bottle of beer in his hand. As I pivot, the bar with its haunting silhouette of prowling wolves dissipates, like a mirage in the desert, swallowed by the stark sterility of our surroundings.

The familiar hum of the morgue reasserts itself as I continue my meal, my gaze once again drawn to the macabre spectacle of burning corpses. "You know, Doc, the contagion is spreading at an alarming speed. Similar incidents are being reported throughout the city," I say, my mind grappling with the horrifying reality unfolding before us. "I'm entangled in a maze of dead ends and misleading clues as I try to solve the enigma of these violent episodes. My thoughts race, searching for any shared factors that could help unravel the inexplicable transformations plaguing our city. But the pieces of the puzzle remain disconnected, leaving me grappling with uncertainty," I confess.

The Doc takes a contemplative swig of his beer, his eyes thoughtful. "It's a tough case, Steve. But remember, sometimes the key to understanding lies hidden in plain sight. Keep searching, and try not to let the enormity of the situation overwhelm you."

In the depths of my dream, I come to the unsettling realization that the key to understanding this sinister epidemic does indeed lie hidden in plain sight. It has to be. The cruel twist of fate has led to my own undoing, placing me in this very state. As the contagion spreads further, its insidious tendrils reach into the heart of the city, and the weight of this discovery bears heavily on me. I yearn to awaken, feeling an urgency to return to consciousness, but I can't pinpoint exactly why. Guilt, maybe? My attempts to rouse myself from this surreal state prove futile, leaving me trapped in the perplexing realm of my dreams.

"Before I forget, Steve," the Doc says abruptly, rising to his feet. I watch in surprise as he grabs a baseball bat and swings it at my shoulder with incredible force. As the impact jolts me, I'm pulled back to the present by the gut-wrenching screams. I'm lying on the ground in a narrow alley at the back of a bar, witnessing the other zombies close in on a motorcyclist who had just hit me with his baseball bat.

The motorcyclist, clad in worn black leather jacket adorned with patches and frayed jeans, valiantly tries to fend off the approaching horde. He swings the bat wildly and shouts, "Get back! Stay away from us!" His girlfriend, dressed in a faded black tank top and torn denim shorts, stands a few feet away from him, frozen with terror and clutching a studded purse.

As the couple's desperate struggle plays out before me, the alley is filled with the chilling sounds of snarling zombies and their own frantic cries. Despite their valiant efforts, the motorcyclist is eventually bitten, and he succumbs to the infection, his once-defiant gaze now vacant and ravenous. His transformation leaves his girlfriend alone and defenseless. She screams in horror, her voice trembling with fear as she desperately calls out her boyfriend's name: "Tom! Tom, please! Help me!" But her pleas fall on deaf ears as the transformed motorcyclist has forgotten his past life and love. The horde descends upon her, and she is devoured mercilessly.

As my body recovers, I can feel some of my bones healing, knitting back together. Despite the pain, I'm still not in control. However, I manage to stand up, my body continuing to roam further with the swarm, as if driven by some unseen force.

My movements feel detached, like watching a marionette's dance through a foggy window. My body, once an extension of my will, is now an entity with its own dark agenda. Every footfall sends a jolt through me, the hard concrete beneath my feet as unfamiliar as the distant moon. My body moves in ways I don't command, like a grotesque puppet in a cruel play, adopting a ghoulish stride amongst the mass of undead. Every so often, a spark of memory flares – as a kid running with my dog in the park, the thrill of chasing after a football in high school. Now, these memories are perverted into a macabre parody, tainted by the horror of my current existence. I hear the rustle of my clothing, the fabric sounding louder, almost alien, as it moves against my skin. Each swish, each scratch, rings out in the cavernous silence of my new reality. A haunting echo of my body's constant, uncontrollable motion.

Each breath I take feels labored, like drawing air through a sheet of lead. My lungs, once vibrant and full of life, now feel like deflated balloons, barely able to perform their function. It's another stark reminder of my changed condition, another piece of my humanity lost to this abominable disease. The night air tastes different now, laced with the sweet stench of panic and despair. It curls around my tongue, teases my senses, whispers monstrous suggestions that I struggle to ignore. Once mundane smells now take on terrifying significance; the tang of sweat, the iron-rich aroma of blood.

Above the chaos, an incongruous sight catches my attention. A lone figure leans casually against the railing of a nearby balcony. In his hand, he holds a bottle of beer. His other hand occupied by a smoldering cigar. He takes a slow sip, completely nonchalant amidst the burgeoning nightmare below. His eyes, seemingly unfazed by the gruesome spectacle, glance over the writhing mass of undead before he raises his bottle in a silent toast to the zombies. The man resumes his casual drinking and smoking, a surreal testament to the apathy and desensitization of some in the face of such unimaginable terror.

We move through the maze of the alleyway and emerge into a hidden playground, nestled unassumingly between the looming city buildings. Bathed in the ethereal glow of the city's streetlight, a little girl, perhaps six or seven, is playing solitarily. She's adorned in a faded, frayed pink dress and a matching ribbon that tames her unkempt hair. In her tiny grip, she clutches a ragged doll, her most cherished companion. Lost in the rhythm of her hopscotch, she remains blissfully unaware of the danger creeping closer with each passing moment.

As an officer, I've encountered this heartbreaking scene many times before: a child left alone on a playground while their parents drink or indulge in their vices, abdicating their responsibilities. In my desperation to warn her, to scream at her to run, my voice fails me. A primal snarl resonates in my throat, raw and shockingly animalistic. It's a sound I barely recognize as my own, a chilling reminder of my transformation. I've become a stranger within my own body, an intruder in a land of savagery and despair.

As the swarm moves closer, I do the only thing I can – I close my eyes, refusing to witness the fate of the innocent child. Yet, her terrified scream pierces my soul, the sound carrying with it unwanted images that flash across my mind. They're vivid and ghastly, each one a testimony to my newfound predatory instincts. It's a mental slideshow of horrors, an intrusive reminder of the monster I've become. When I gather the courage to open my eyes again, I see the little girl among the crowd. Her innocence is lost, as she shuffles alongside the other zombies, her once-cherished doll still clutched in her hand.

As we emerge from the alley onto the main road, a man dressed in an expensive, business-like suit, giving the impression of a wealthy businessman, frantically tries to outrun the horde on his electric scooter. Sweat drips down his face as he glances back, urging his scooter to go faster. "Come on, come on, you overpriced piece of junk!" he shouts, leaning forward as if the extra effort might push his scooter beyond its limits, like a desperate rider spurring on a tired horse. There's something familiar about his face, but I can't quite place him in my memories. I have a vague feeling that I might have met him in the past, and the encounter wasn't particularly pleasant. His appearance brings to mind the image of a repulsive palm crawler, though I can't quite pinpoint why I feel this way upon seeing him.

For a moment, it seems as if he might succeed in his desperate escape. But then, the scooter's battery drains, and it comes to a sudden, heart-stopping halt. Panicked, he looks down at the lifeless scooter and curses his bad luck. "You've got to be kidding me! Not now, not now!" he exclaims, urgency evident in his voice. His plea goes unanswered as the horde catches up to him. He is bitten and, with a final scream of anguish, succumbs to the infection and joins the mass of undead.

Unwavering in their pursuit of human flesh, the living dead march forward, their disfigured forms casting twisted shadows on the desolate streets. From a dark, narrow alley, a man emerges, fancying himself a real-life Rambo. Armed and seemingly ready to face the unstoppable tide of the living dead, he exudes an air of grim determination. Inspired by his silver screen idols, he steadies his weapon and takes aim at the approaching mass of reanimated corpses. With a smirk, he calls out, "Welcome to hell, zombies! Time to send you back where you came from!" His words create a chilling display of fear and defiance amidst the chaos.

His bravado, however, is betrayed by his inexperience, masked beneath a veneer of false confidence. As the wave of living dead steadily closes in, their grotesque forms illuminated by streetlights, he forgets a crucial step—disengaging the safety on his weapon. He pulls the trigger, expecting a hail of bullets to cut through the night, only to be met with the hollow click-click of his futile attempt.

"No, no, no!" he cries out in dread, frantically fumbling with his weapon as the realization of his error dawns on him far too late. His face contorts with terror as the zombies swarm him. "This can't be real!" Helpless and overwhelmed, he is swiftly bitten and assimilated into the ravenous mob. Within moments, the man who once sought to defy the apocalypse is transformed into one of its harbingers. His dreams of heroism snuffed out, replaced by an insatiable hunger for human flesh as he joins the ranks of the damned.

The zombie swarm swells menacingly with each passing second, the addition of new victims fueling its horrific expansion. The scene of carnage escalates further as I witness more lives being abruptly extinguished. Amid the chaos, an elderly couple catches my attention. They hold each other tightly, eyes closed, as if ready to welcome their inevitable fate. Their embrace speaks volumes of their lifelong love and companionship, tragically coming to an end at the hands of the undead multitude.

Meanwhile, a young couple is desperately trying to escape, their hands clutched together as they try to weave through the chaos. Yet, the approaching swarm is unyielding, and their fate seems sealed. Behind them, an elderly man stumbles and falls, his eyes wide with terror. His voice cracks with desperation as he calls out, "Help me, please... don't leave me here!" His plea echoes hauntingly through the turmoil, underscoring the grim reality of humanity's desperate plight.

My monstrous heart tightens in my chest, a lingering vestige of my humanity aching at the sight of these innocent lives in torment. Their anguished cries cut through the air, ensnaring them in this nightmarish reality—some being devoured alive, while others are unwillingly assimilated into the legion of the living dead. I attempt to close my eyes, seeking a moment of respite from the horror that unfolds around me. But they refuse to obey, remaining lidless and unblinking. It's as if the virus itself forces them open, intent on torturing me and forcing me to bear witness to every moment of this macabre spectacle.

A frantic mother pounds on the locked door of an upscale art gallery, her voice shrill with panic, "Por favor, let us in! Dios mío, save my child!" Her desperate pleas echo off the walls, yet they are met with cold indifference. Behind the glass, the gallery patrons, some still nursing their champagne flutes, merely observe the unfolding spectacle with morbid amusement. The frightened child clings even tighter to the mother, their small body trembling, their tears cutting through the grime on their cheeks. Some patrons even film the horrific scene, their phones casting an eerie glow on the despair outside.

Among the onlookers, I spot a familiar face – Mayor Ortega, a prominent figure in the city's political landscape. She stands surrounded by an array of carefully packed paintings, luxury acquisitions from the gallery. These artifacts of wealth serve as an undeniable testament to the privilege she enjoys at the taxpayers' expense. Her eyes, devoid of empathy, coldly survey the chaos unfolding outside the locked doors of the gallery.

As one of the terrified patrons musters the courage to approach the door, fingers trembling towards the lock, I see Mayor Ortega's lips move sternly. Even through the soundproof glass, I manage to read her lips, her harsh command slicing through the chaos as if I can hear her, "Stop him! Don't let him open that door! Shoot him if need be!"

Without a moment's hesitation, one of her bodyguards obeys, the echo of the gunshot ringing out starkly against the tumultuous sounds outside. The hapless civilian drops lifelessly, a blossom of red splattering across the reinforced glass door. The bullet, however, doesn't stop there; it strikes the door, leaving a spider-web of cracks radiating from the impact point.

On the other side of the reinforced glass, the terrified mother and her child witness the brutal execution unfold. The mother's face, initially frozen in shock, transforms into an expression of determination. In contrast, her child's face remains a mask of innocent terror. Summoning a surge of strength, the mother scoops up her child and darts away from the hellish scene.

The approaching horde soon descends upon the art gallery. The first wave of zombies, seemingly undistracted by the fleeing pair, focuses their relentless onslaught on the gallery's entrance, inadvertently granting the desperate duo a small window of opportunity to slip away.

Inside the gallery, the once-confident customers cower in terror as the nightmare they had been observing through the glass now threatens to consume them. Yet, amidst the chaos, one patron, with a champagne flute in one hand, clings determinedly to his phone with the other, resolved to capture the horrifying events as they unfold.

As the siege intensifies, several zombies suddenly break away from the main group and start chasing the fleeing mother and child. From a distance, I can see the fear in the tearful child's eyes as he watches me. He is scared of me, scared of all of us.

Just then, a burly construction worker, garbed in a high-visibility vest speckled with dirt and sweat, emerges from a hinged manhole. His rugged face is set in a determined grimace, a hard hat sitting low over his furrowed brow. His once-white work pants bear the telltale signs of a day's labor, stained with dust and grime. Shock registers on his face as he takes in the scene of carnage, but his instincts quickly kick in.

Understanding the urgency of the situation, he spots the terrified mother and child, and urgently calls out to them, "Hey, over here! Hurry!" His voice, rough from years of yelling over the din of construction machinery, pierces the tumultuous scene with a startling clarity. The mother's gaze follows the construction worker's voice, and she notices the open manhole and the road maintenance vehicle with its glowing orange beacon, offering a glimmer of hope amidst the chaos.

With a haste that mirrors the escalating chaos, the construction worker steps up to the edge of the manhole. He extends his sturdy, calloused hands to the mother, aiding her and the child into the dimly lit refuge below. As they descend, the mother clings tightly to her child. The construction worker follows suit, descending into the manhole. He pulls the heavy cover over the opening, the hinged design allowing him to secure it from below. The timing is impeccable; just as the cover seals them in, the first of the split-off zombies arrives, its gnarled hands clawing at the now impenetrable surface of the manhole.

Abruptly, the piercing sound of shattering glass reverberates through the street, soon accompanied by a chorus of horrifying screams. Carried forward by the unstoppable tide of the undead, I'm thrust into the heart of the art gallery, once a pristine sanctuary now tainted by carnage. The panicked cries form a chaotic symphony, blending with the dissonant crashes of sculptures toppling, paintings being torn from the walls, and champagne bottles shattering on the marble floor. The gallery's destruction culminates in a crescendo of chaos, reducing its once lofty elegance to a scene of grisly devastation.

Inside, the privileged patrons, once safe behind the locked door, are now the helpless victims of the nightmare they had been observing from the safety of their glass fortress. Some are consumed instantly, their lives extinguished brutally and without mercy. The savage spectacle sends splatters of blood and viscera onto the obscenely expensive paintings that adorn the gallery walls

- abstract pieces that only the most pretentious art snobs could claim to understand.

Others succumb to the ravenous horde's gnashing teeth and slashing claws, their agonized convulsions adding a horrifying detail to the gruesome spectacle. Abandoned to their suffering, these unfortunate individuals are destined to become the latest recruits to our ever-swelling ranks.

Each ragged breath brings a miasma of scents, a cocktail of fear and despair, underlaid by the alluring aroma of human flesh. It's nauseating, revolting, yet undeniably tempting. I push back against the urge, a silent protest lodged within the confines of my diseased mind.

I resist. God, how I resist. Every ounce of my willpower goes into suppressing the savage urges. The sight of a person no longer registers as a fellow human, but rather, an object of primal hunger. I'm trying to ignore the salivating impulse. The war within me is ceaseless, exhausting, like trying to hold back a tidal wave with a dam made of sand.

As chaos unfolds around us, the sharp report of gunfire rings out, most likely Mayor Ortega's bodyguards, desperately trying to carve a path through the undead to the sleek, black armored vehicle parked across the street. Through the turmoil, I see the Mayor, her face a mask of hysteria, screaming orders at her bodyguards, "Save me, you imbeciles! Your lives are expendable! My life is the one that matters!" Yet, despite her commands and their efforts, the crescendo of terrified screams paints a grim picture - they never reach the supposed safety of the vehicle.

As the gallery descends into chaos, a notably vibrant figure stands out. A man, his head adorned with a crown of afro hair, who in life was clearly an art connoisseur of the highest order, grapples with one of my fellow undead. His garish attire, featuring high-heeled shoes, a flamboyant purple boa, and a matching eccentric hat, creates a stark spectacle amid the frenzied disorder.

The art snob's eyes widen in terror as the zombie's teeth sink into his neck, his desperate pleas for mercy interrupted by a choked gasp, "Mon Dieu, not the cashmere!" In a gruesome display of inevitability, he's pushed to the gallery's cold marble floor, his struggles growing weaker by the second.

After a few agonizing moments, his struggles cease. Yet, the peace of death is a luxury not afforded to him. Within seconds, his body jerks back to life, the newly-turned zombie clumsily rises to his feet. Breaking into the frenzied pace of the horde, he stumbles forward with an uncanny sense of urgency. For a moment, his rigid hands continue to clutch his shattered champagne glass and phone, until they inevitably fall to the ground. His first steps into undeath are taken in the extravagant high-heels he wore in life, a grotesque parody of his former self.

As the final, chilling screams emanating from the gallery begin to fade, swallowed by the night, the focus of the insatiable crowd shifts. They spill out onto the streets like a tidal wave of death, their predatory senses honed in on the remaining souls who hadn't been lucky enough to secure sanctuary.

A homeless man, swathed in worn-out layers of clothing, takes refuge in a narrow, grimy alleyway. He's discovered all too soon. As the reanimated creatures approach, their menacing snarls reverberating off the graffiti-covered walls, he musters a feeble plea, "No... please... I... I ain't got nothin'..." His voice trails off, swallowed by the predatory sounds of the encroaching mob.

In the center of the street, a wheelchair-bound man, his legs mere stumps, desperately attempts to propel himself to safety. His nurse, who had been pushing him, falls prey to the reanimated horrors first, her screams of terror reverberating through the chaos. His eyes widen in horror as the undead creatures close in on him, their teeth sinking into his flesh. In mere moments, he undergoes the horrifying transformation. Toppling from his wheelchair, the newly-turned creature drags itself on the ground, its previous disability no longer a deterrent in its relentless pursuit for human flesh.

Not far away, an elderly woman, her frail form weighed down by a bag of groceries, stumbles in her haste to escape. As she falls, the bag bursts open, sending apples, oranges, and a medley of other fruits and vegetables rolling across the pavement. Her fall signals the end, and the creatures descend upon her like vultures, her pleas for mercy disappearing amidst the tumultuous roar of the undead.

In the shadowy recesses of an alleyway, a fentanyl addict stumbles aimlessly. His uncoordinated movements and vacant expression make him almost indistinguishable from the creatures that haunt the streets. His gaunt, shirtless figure, shrouded by a long, unkempt beard, bears the harsh toll of his addiction. Suddenly, the walking dead descend upon him. The bite they deliver hardly seems to affect him at first. His already lifeless expression remains unchanged, but then his movements become more purposeful, more driven. The transformation is subtly disturbing. His eyes, once dull and vacant, are now unnerving orbs glowing with an eerie orange hue. The beast he has become is barely discernible from the ghost of a man lost to the tenacious grip of fentanyl, an eerie foreshadowing of his grim fate.

Further down the street, a street musician finds himself backed against a cold, brick wall. His beloved guitar lays discarded on the pavement, the haunting melodies he'd been playing earlier now replaced by a discordant symphony of his own terrified screams. The night, once filled with the vibrant rhythm of the city, is now a chilling soundtrack of humanity's downfall.

As the swarm continues its grim march, the pervasive violence and horrific scenes become too overwhelming to bear. Succumbing to the sheer force of my will, my eyes finally clamp shut, providing a fleeting escape from the horrifying reality that surrounds me. The discordant symphony of screams and cries of terror persist, echoing through my consciousness. Yet, as the moments pass, these sounds of horror slowly recede, their intensity fading like the gradual transition from wakefulness to sleep. Despite the external chaos, my inner world retreats into the hazy realm of a fevered dream.

3

A wave of yearning washes over me as recollections of the life I once shared with my girlfriend rise from the recesses of my mind. A strange scene unfolds before me, set in a room that is an amalgamation of a bar, our dining room with a grandfather clock, and a park bathed in golden sunlight. We sit at a table, attempting to eat a meal with an odd assortment of utensils – using a saw to cut our food and a hammer to keep the shape-shifting hamburger in place on the plate. The scene feels like a chaotic fusion of two or three different events or memories, melding into one bizarre experience.

As the fever dream shifts and morphs, Sarah's voice, soothing as a melody, emerges from the haze. "Remember when we spent the whole day in bed, just talking and laughing?" I reply with a gentle, facetious tone, "Of course I remember, my dearest Sarah." I strain to remember the sound of my own laughter, the feel of a smile gracing my face. Yet, such memories feel alien, a distant echo from a life that I barely recognize as my own. The memory of lazy weekend mornings with her by my side comes into focus. We luxuriate in each other's embrace, the aroma of freshly brewed coffee mingling with the tender touch of sunlight streaming through the windows.

Our dreamy surroundings change once again, and we find ourselves hand in hand, roaming the city streets and discovering hidden treasures. The scene transitions to nightfall, and we're curled up together on the couch, our bodies entwined as we surrender to the mesmerizing flicker of our favorite movies and shows.

But the fever dream doesn't shy away from the challenges our love has faced. "You always do this! Why can't you just admit when you're wrong?" I shout in the dream, the frustration in my voice evident.

In response, Sarah's voice, calm and reassuring, echoes in the dream. "Despite the disagreements, we always find a way to make it through, don't we? We learn and grow together, and our love only gets stronger." Her words remind me that, time and time again, we emerge from these conflicts with a renewed sense of unity and understanding.

As her soothing words fade, the dream shifts and takes on a surreal quality. The people around us become a blur, unrecognizable and frozen, as if time has come to a standstill. Only Sarah and I remain in motion, along with something sinister and ominous in the distance. A horrifying, ravenous creature, craving our flesh, advances towards us on the street, and I instantly recognize the danger. I draw my pistol to protect her, but the zombie proves swifter. Placing myself between them, I yell at Sarah, "Run!" I shove her away, striving to shield her from any harm.

I feel the searing pain of the zombie's bite, sealing my fate. The anguish of knowing I will lose her and the life we've so carefully built together is unbearable. Summoning the last of my strength, I grip my pistol tightly, my finger trembling on the trigger. With a deafening blast, the bullet erupts from the barrel, tearing through the attacker zombie's chin and rocketing upward into its head. The creature's skull splits open with a sickening crunch, showering gore in all directions as it collapses to the ground. As the lifeless body crumples before me, the virus begins to overtake my system.

The dream then morphs, blurring the edges of reality and fantasy as I find myself transported to a more tender, loving moment. We stand together in a large, dimly lit space that is an uncanny fusion of a dance hall and a dining room, the walls bleeding gently as if weeping for the love we've lost. A piano plays softly in the corner, its keys moving on their own, creating a haunting melody that envelops us. As we dance gracefully, our bodies sway in perfect harmony. The warm embrace of her arms wraps around me, and her eyes meet mine, filled with love and adoration. "I love you," she whispers, her voice barely audible over the melancholic tune. The world beyond our embrace fades away, leaving only the two of us in this intimate, dreamlike haven.

As we continue to dance, she gently rests her hand on my upper arm, holding me close. Her touch is tender at first, but soon her grip begins to tighten. Her fingers press into my flesh, gradually digging deeper and deeper as the pressure increases. I look into her eyes, searching for an explanation for her sudden grip, but her gaze remains unchanged – full of love and compassion. The pain intensifies as her fingers carve into my arm, the sensation all-consuming. I try to pull away, but her grip remains unyielding. Panic begins to set in as I struggle to break free, my mind racing to comprehend the bizarre turn of events.

My eyes snap open, and I'm jolted back to the grim reality surrounding me. A stray bullet tore into my upper arm, and despite the searing pain, I recall the sensation from my days as a police officer. Now, instead of battling for my life, I'm an unwilling participant in the unrelenting hunt for the living. The pain momentarily distracts me, and I realize that if it weren't for my unwavering focus on hanging onto my memories, I'd surely go mad in this nightmarish reality. I cling to this inner struggle as my last bastion of sanity.

Unseen chains drag me along with the rest of the zombie swarm, my body moving in grotesque synchrony with the others. I'm a marionette, my strings yanked by the insidious pathogen coursing through my veins. The struggle for control is exhausting, a constant battle that leaves me mentally drained and despairing.

The sounds of the city, once a comforting symphony of life, are now filled with the voices of terror. The blaring horns, the frantic shouts, the desperate sobs—they cut through the cold silence like hot knives. Each one a stark reminder of the humanity I'm losing grip of.

I survey the burning vehicles and countless bodies strewn across the streets, a stark portrayal of the city's catastrophic downfall. What was once a bustling metropolis now lies in ruins, a graveyard of shattered dreams and extinguished lives. I find myself amidst a zombie swarm of around sixty, their ranks swelling unstoppably as each newly infected victim succumbs to the ravenous hunger that drives the walking dead. A scent wafts through the air, sweet and intoxicating, yet horrifying in its allure. It's the smell of life, of humans, and my diseased brain translates it into one word - food.

As I survey the scene, I recognize the 63rd Street Kings, a notorious gang known for their distinct purple head scarves and a menacing crown tattoo on their necks, fighting back against the advancing wave of the undead. Men and women alike, it seems even the wives of the gang members are taking their part in the action, standing shoulder to shoulder with their partners in the face of the zombie menace. Among them is their hefty member, Lil' Rascal, a drug dealer I had arrested numerous times in the past. To my surprise, he and his fellow gang members are now herding children into vans for evacuation, while simultaneously engaging the creatures with their pistols and submachine guns.

Zombies lunge at the gang members, their gnarled hands grasping for a taste of living flesh. The 63rd Street Kings move with impressive agility, dodging and pushing the advancing monsters away as they continue to fire their weapons. Though it's clear that they're not sharpshooters, holding their golden-plated and other fancy pistols in a gangster-style grip that results in more misses than hits, their determination and continuous assault manage to keep the undead at bay. Most zombies are struck in the body, only to stagger momentarily before resuming their pursuit. Those few enough to be shot in the head, however, crumple lifelessly to the ground, their nightmarish existence finally extinguished. Gradually, I realize that my wound is slowly healing—an unsettling reminder of the unnatural state I now inhabit.

"Yo, hurry up, man! Get 'em in the van!" Lil' Rascal yells, his voice strained with urgency. The other gang members shout and fire on the encroaching reanimated beings. "We ain't leavin' our fam behind!" one of them declares, his gun blazing as he narrowly avoids being bitten.

Lil' Rascal expertly aims his tactical shotgun and fires, delivering a precise headshot to the art snob zombie that had come dangerously close to one of the children. "Sorry, fancy brother, this ain't your show!" he quips as the undead creature collapses to the ground, no longer a threat.

Among the gang members, I spot Rosa Martinez, no longer in her police uniform. Memories of the incident under the bridge, which led to her discharge from the force, begin to resurface in my mind. A crusade led by NGOs had broken her career, causing her to lose both her job and her home. It seems the rumors were true that the 63rd took good care of her, helping her after she had done so much for the community during her time with the police.

Now, wielding a shotgun, Rosa Martinez battles the zombies alongside the gang members. Curiously, it appears to be the same weapon she used against the perpetrator under the bridge – a shotgun that mysteriously vanished from the evidence locker following the trial – and now serves to defend the people here.

Rosa shoots the zombies with resolve and professionalism, her skill and training evident in her precise aim. After taking down several reanimated corpses, she calls out to the others, "I'm empty!" Hearing her, the gang members immediately form a protective barrier in front of her while she swiftly reloads. Once her shotgun is ready, she returns to the front line and continues to fire, providing crucial support to the group as they battle the swarm.

As the zombie in the rich business suit comes face to face with Martinez, a sudden realization hits me. This was the corrupt judge who had attempted to send her to jail despite knowing she had done the right thing. Rumors had it that he was bribed by certain NGOs. It was only due to the district captain's intervention that her sentence had been suspended.

When Martinez spots the once-judge, now a hideous zombie, anger flashes across her face. She steps out of line and hurries in front of him, aiming her shotgun. The weapon clicks, empty. The tension mounts as the zombie lunges towards her, but Martinez reacts with lightning speed, striking his head with the butt of her shotgun, causing him to stagger back. In the blink of an eye, she loads a single cartridge into the weapon, quickly aims, and fires, taking him down with a well-deserved headshot.

As Martinez rejoins the line of defenders, the others look at her with respect. One of them nods approvingly and says in a rough voice, "Revenge served cold, girl. Nice shot." With a sense of satisfaction, she continues fighting alongside her newfound allies. I can't help but think that this was true justice, something that Martinez had long been owed.

As the vans fill up with children, the situation grows increasingly tense. The horde threatens to overpower the group, but they hold their ground, ensuring the last of the children are safely inside the vehicles. With the vans loaded, the gang members start to retreat, covering each other's backs as they make their escape.

Lil' Rascal is about to board the last van when he spots a woman still struggling to reach safety. Instead of abandoning his neighbors in the face of danger, he stays true to his word and protects those he considers family.

"Ayo, girl, take my spot! Y'all get outta here!" Lil' Rascal shouts in his distinct slang, making sure the woman gets on the van.

"I'ma hold 'em off, buy y'all some time!" In that moment, Lil' Rascal redeems himself in my eyes.

Seeing Lil' Rascal's sacrifice, a young man, who can't be more than eighteen, sitting in the front passenger seat of the van gets out, and shouts to Rosa. "Yo, Flutter! You gotta take my spot 'n protect the fam!" He readies himself to join Lil' Rascal in the fight against the zombies, speaking with a similar slang.

Martinez hesitates for a moment, glancing back at the zombies closing in. She quickly empties all the remaining rounds of her shotgun into the mob of undead before nodding resolutely. As the door of the van closes behind her, she starts to reload her shotgun. That's when she catches sight of me in my zombified state. Surprise flashes across her face, and I can clearly see her mouth the word, "No."

As the van backs away from the zombie onslaught, Rosa leans out the window, shotgun in hand, trying to get a clear shot at me. Her face is a mix of determination and pain. But she hesitates. I watch as the distance between us grows, and I realize that she couldn't bring herself to pull the trigger. Rosa retreats back into her seat, lowering her shotgun. She drops her head back and I read her lips, mouthing the words, "Damn it, Steve!" In a swift motion, the van makes a quick 180-degree turn and speeds away, its wheels screeching against the pavement.

As all the vans race away, Lil' Rascal's voice cuts through the chaos, resolve etched on his face. "Quick, everyone, into that crib! We'll make our stand there."

The survivors hastily make their way into the crib, a multi-storied residential building with its sturdy iron gate. Once inside, they secure the gate behind them. Zombies press against the fence, their gnarled hands reaching through the gaps, craving flesh. Two gang members, one of them the young guy who bravely gave up his spot for Rosa, fire at the approaching horde to hold them back. Trapped in the zombie form, I find myself dangerously close to the front line of the undead, nervously anticipating a stray bullet with my name on it.

Lil' Rascal addresses the group, rallying their spirits. "Aight, y'all, listen up! We gotta fight 'em off, keep 'em busy, and make our escape! I know we ain't all soldiers, but we got heart, and we got each other. Let's do this!"

Though they manage to take down a few zombies, they know the fence won't last long. The young guy shouts back, "Yo, Rascal, time to move, man! These dawgs ain't gonna stop!"

The fences creak and groan under the assault of the zombies. It's clear they won't hold much longer. As the reanimated corpses start to break through, Lil' Rascal and the survivors quickly adapt their strategy. They lead the zombies into the narrow corridors and tight spaces within the house, hoping to limit the number of creatures they have to face at any given time.

"Keep movin', y'all! Lead 'em into the tight spots, we can hold 'em off there!" Lil' Rascal shouts, urging the survivors to retreat deeper into the house.

The sounds of gunfire are punctuated by fervent shouts and rallying cries as they bravely strive to hold their line and protect one another. Some zombies take a bullet to the skull and tumble down, lifeless. Shots zip past me, one skimming alarmingly close to my head, while another burrows through my body, triggering an acute pain that swiftly subsides as my wound regenerates.

"Keep 'em off, Ty!" one of them shouts, his voice thick with tenacity and fear.

"Watch yo' back, D!" another one yells, his accent strong as he warns his comrade of an approaching zombie.

"Right side, right side!" someone warns, directing attention to a new wave of zombie attackers.

The survivors skillfully lure us up a staircase, taking intermittent shots at the mass of undead. Yet, the swarm appears invincible, and as the defenders' ammunition supply diminishes, their escape routes become alarmingly limited. Inevitably, they are apprehended one after another, meeting a gruesome fate—either devoured or converted into one of us.

The unstoppable pull of the horde is like a tide, sweeping me along in its grisly current. I feel some strange comfort in their unity, in their single-minded purpose. But the familiarity of it only heightens my horror - I'm part of them, yet desperately striving to separate my consciousness from the monstrous collective.

As the living dead multitude ceaselessly grows, it now encompasses a man donning vibrant football gear—presumably hoping it would shield him—a postal worker clad in his uniform with his mail bag still slung across his shoulder, and an elderly security guard wearing lackluster gear, who likely took the job to augment his modest pension.

As I contemplate the staggering population of the metropolitan area—approximately four million souls, encompassing the city and its outskirts—I am gripped by the horrifying realization of the sheer number of potential victims that could bolster the undead army's ranks. The thought strikes me with a profound sense of dread, for if left unchecked, this monstrosity could swell into an unstoppable force of devastation, consuming every last remnant of humanity in its path. Each of these individuals, who once led ordinary lives with dreams and aspirations, could become unwilling participants in the nightmarish existence of the undead.

As we descend to the ground level, following Lil' Rascal and the survivors who desperately try to find a way out, I find myself acutely aware of the icy embrace of the night, the frigid air seeping into my decaying flesh. It's as if my numb body is beginning to awaken from its torpid state, responding to the bitter chill that envelops me. The night's darkness engulfs the desolate streets, casting eerie shadows that dance and twist, heightening the sense of dread that pervades the atmosphere.

Suddenly, a worn-out school bus, its once vibrant yellow paint faded and peeling, screeches to a halt near Lil' Rascal and the remaining survivors. They scramble aboard, narrowly evading the encroaching zombie horde. Among the last to board is the young man who'd given up his place to Rosa, his pursuer hot on his heels. The zombie, distinguishable as the earlier jogger, his hand still clutching an ArcticAde bottle, lunges at him. Just in the nick of time, Lil' Rascal raises his shotgun and, with deadly accuracy, obliterates the creature's head in a grisly spray of gore. The jogger-zombie falls, the ArcticAde bottle tumbling from his lifeless grip.

"Yo, I'm empty! Need more shells!" Lil' Rascal shouts, not realizing that the young man he defended has already been bitten. As the bus driver, an older man with rasta hair, slams the door shut, the bitten survivor turns and begins to attack everyone inside with a spine-chilling ferocity.

From a distance, I can see the flashes of gunfire illuminating the bus windows as the night sky casts an ominous gloom over the desolate streets. My body moves uncontrolled further, and the bus slips out of my sight. I still hear the sounds of gunshots and screams emanating from the bus, but they gradually fade into the distance. The incessant march of the undead drowns out all other noise, our collective moans and shuffling steps echoing hauntingly through the forsaken streets. The uncertainty of Lil' Rascal and the other survivors' fates gnaws at me, but with my body still under the influence of the virus, I have no choice but to press on with the horde as it dictates.

As the cold air stirs my senses, I become increasingly aware of the smells that surround me. The once-dulled scents now sharpen, revealing an array of odors that assault my nostrils. The pungent stench of decay mingles with the acrid scent of smoke from the smoldering ruins nearby. Amidst the olfactory chaos, fainter scents emerge—fear, desperation, and even the lingering fragrance of a once-familiar perfume, all blending together into a hauntingly dissonant symphony.

The horde's pace mysteriously decelerates, its members lingering as if attempting to detect the aroma of new quarry. In these moments of relative tranquility, I can't help but speculate whether there are others like me—imprisoned within their monstrous guises, desperately clinging to their humanity, and seeking a way to liberate themselves from this living nightmare.

As I persist in observing the swarm's movements, I wrestle with the conundrum of what drives us as a whole. Despite our zombie state rendering us unable to communicate conventionally, we progress in harmony, as if guided by a communal, primal instinct. This mysterious influence binds us together, propelling us unyieldingly forward in our tireless hunt for the living.

The stagnant air brims with anticipation, as if the very night itself holds its breath, awaiting our next move. A smell wafts into my nostrils, the scent of life, of humanity. It's intoxicating, terrifyingly so. My mind recoils in horror, while my corrupted senses greedily soak in the aroma, highlighting the rift this affliction has torn into my being. Slowly, the horde comes to life, lured by the scent of fresh victims. The communal hunger of the undead swells, a ravenous, insatiable yearning that ceaselessly drives us forward.

As the zombie swarm marches toward the downtown, I can feel the fever burning within me, fighting for control. The virus courses through my veins like molten fire, seeking to consume every last vestige of my humanity. My muscles ache with a dull, throbbing pain, and my vision blurs at the edges, as if my own body is rebelling against my will. The feverish heat radiates from within, threatening to engulf me in its inescapable embrace.

It's a constant battle, a precarious dance on the edge of oblivion, as I struggle to hold onto the fraying threads of my human existence amidst the chaos and the darkness that surrounds me. As my consciousness fades, the horde pulses forward, undeterred by the encroaching shadows, seemingly oblivious to my wavering grip on reality.

4

In the depths of a surreal nightmare, I find myself wandering through a seemingly infinite house, its endless corridors and rooms melding together in a disorienting labyrinth. The walls are decorated with eerie crime scene photographs from my past cases, their gruesome imagery evoking a haunting sense of familiarity. Each doorway I pass through reveals yet another room filled with distorted memories and echoes of my life as a detective and Sarah's boyfriend.

One room plunges me into a twisted version of our first date, where we share a candlelit dinner amidst the unnerving presence of lifeless mannequins, their unblinking eyes fixated on us. Another room transports me to a crime scene where Sarah appears as the victim, her lifeless form distorted and contorted in an unnatural manner, a grim reflection of my deepest fears.

As I navigate this nightmarish labyrinth, the house appears to pulsate with a malevolent life of its own. The walls contort and shift, drawing me deeper into the heart of darkness. I stumble into a chamber where my past cases and Sarah's memories meld in a macabre dance. The victims and the undead move together in a grim spectacle of sorrow and horror.

Yearning to flee the intensifying phantasmagoria, I at last find a room radiating an illusion of normalcy. The familiar sight of our cozy kitchen, bathed in the soft glow of morning sunlight, provides a stark contrast to the surreal terror I've just traversed. Sarah stands at the counter, her back to me as she hums a familiar tune, seemingly unaware of the grotesque horrors lurking beyond the kitchen's threshold. Her hands move expertly as she prepares a pizza, kneading the dough with practiced ease. This scene provides a fleeting moment of solace and comfort amidst the chaos of my bewildering dream world.

As Sarah works on the pizza, she announces cheerfully, "We have guests for dinner tonight!" I glance around and realize the kitchen has seamlessly merged with the dining room, creating a disconcerting amalgamation of the two spaces. At the table, a group of zombies sit patiently, their lifeless eyes aglow with an eerie orange hue, fixated on Sarah and her culinary preparations. A shiver of unease grips me as I can't decide whether they are waiting for the pizza or eager to devour Sarah herself.

Sarah kneads the dough further, her movements fluid and graceful. She spreads the tomato sauce evenly across the surface, then generously sprinkles a blend of mozzarella and cheddar cheese over it. With a practiced hand, she artfully arranges a colorful medley of toppings: pepperoni slices, bell peppers, red onions, mushrooms, black olives, and juicy pineapple chunks. Her every action displays her love for cooking and baking, as she creates a mouthwatering masterpiece in the midst of chaos.

The zombies, their gruesome features softened by the dreamlike haze, watch in fascination as Sarah works her culinary magic, a scene that is at once comforting and deeply unsettling. As she searches for the saltshaker, the zombies' anticipation appears to grow, their restless movements mirroring my own mounting anxiety.

Finding the saltshaker, she seasons the pizza before moving on to the final, horrifying step. With an unnervingly serene smile, Sarah begins to slice her own fingers, severing them as if they were sausages, and placing them delicately onto the pizza.

I watch in horror, unable to tear my eyes away from the gruesome display, as the pizza is completed, adorned with Sarah's own mutilated fingers. The waiting zombies grow increasingly restless, their hunger and anticipation tangible in the air. And yet, through it all, Sarah's smile never wavers, illustrating the depths of surrealism and terror that have taken hold in this twisted nightmare.

With a flourish, Sarah opens the oven to place the pizza inside. However, as the oven door swings open, it reveals a terrifying sight – the interior resembles a crematorium, the fiery flames licking at the edges, eager to consume whatever is placed within. Undeterred, Sarah slides the grisly pizza into the oven, the heat casting an eerie glow on her face as she closes the door, sealing the grotesque dish inside. "Almost ready," she says cheerfully, her voice strikingly at odds with the horrifying scene unfolding before my eyes.

Sarah walks towards me, her fingers miraculously restored, defying all logic and the bounds of reality. She takes my hand gently, her touch warm and familiar despite the unsettling scene that just transpired. "Before dinner, I want to show you something," she whispers, her voice a haunting echo of the woman I once knew.

In an instant, we find ourselves in a distorted, surreal bathroom. The warped tiles bend and twist, as if struggling to maintain their form, and the once gleaming fixtures are tarnished, marred by an unseen darkness. The room pulses with an unsettling energy, the air thick with an unspoken dread.

Sarah leads me to the mirror, her grip tightening as she urges me to face my reflection. My heart lurches in my chest as I see my true zombie self staring back at me, the disturbing visage a stark reminder of the monstrous fate I have endured. But something is amiss—the eerie glow in my demented eyes begins to fade, as though my humanity is trying to reassert itself. "Look at yourself," she sneers, her voice dripping with contempt. "See how ugly you are, trying to resist what you've become!"

Suddenly, Sarah screams in anger, her face contorted with rage. "I hate you!" she snarls, her voice laden with venom. Without warning, she grabs my head and violently smashes it into the mirror, shattering the glass and plunging me deeper into the nightmare's twisted embrace.

Abruptly, I am jolted back to reality as my body crashes through a window and into a shopping plaza, hot on the heels of survivors. The swarm floods the mall, their ravenous hunger driving them relentlessly forward. We're no longer merely jogging but propelling ourselves with startling swiftness, our pace far more rapid than ever before. I'm a puppet with the virus as my puppeteer, commanding my body with ruthless efficiency. My limbs jerk and twist, moving with a life of their own. It's an eerie ballet of the damned, one that I'm a reluctant dancer in.

The scene is made all the more chilling by the music blaring from the social justice warrior zombie's headphones—an unsettlingly upbeat rendition of Mozart's Dies Irae. I recognize the music, as Sarah had a deep love for the classics, ranging from Mozart to Bach. She even collected vinyl records of the classical greats, preferring them to CDs or MP3s. The haunting melody serves as an eerie soundtrack to the carnage unfolding before me.

The survivors, an eclectic group of individuals, are each fighting for their lives against the relentless undead onslaught. Among them are a hot-dog vendor armed with a makeshift umbrella spear, a pizza delivery guy wielding a sharpened mop handle, and a fitness instructor clutching a golf club. There's also a food court chef brandishing a razor-sharp katana and several security guards. Some of the guards are employing pistols while others use tasers against the ravenous horde. These survivors have armored themselves with fast-food plastic trays, cut precisely and strapped onto their hands and legs for protection. Some have even fashioned patchwork shields from tabletops and other materials, providing an additional defense layer against their seemingly unstoppable attackers.

The most striking sight, however, is a trio of Roman soldier cosplayers. One is clad as a Roman Praetorian Centurion, standing out in beautifully detailed black armor and a distinct helmet adorned with a black horsehair crest. His two companions are dressed as Roman Legionaries from the XV Legion, identifiable by the emblems on their red shields. These Roman history enthusiasts stand as the defensive spearhead at the choke point, forming a disciplined formation with their scutum shields and gladius swords at the ready.

A praetorian steps forward, forcefully shoving back a zombie with his shield before spinning around to drive his sword into the creature's skull. Meanwhile, a legionary pins another attacker to the wall with his shield, following with calculated, lethal thrusts of his gladius. The third soldier targets low, deftly slicing through the legs of an advancing zombie before driving his blade into its cranium. Despite the surrounding chaos, these faux soldiers maintain their formation, their swords flashing like deadly scorpions' stingers.

Behind the disciplined Roman cosplayers, the other survivors stand firm. The hot-dog vendor and fitness instructor manage to crush zombie skulls with their umbrella spear and golf club. Meanwhile, a nurse, a courier guy, and a well-dressed lady, potentially a jewelry store manager, utilize makeshift weapons made from scavenged gardening tools. Enhanced with nails and other sharp elements, these modified tools serve as deadly weapons in their desperate fight for survival.

A store assistant, having found an expensive chainsaw in a nearby hardware store, brandishes it menacingly, the price tag still dangling from the handle. Demonstrating a deep understanding of his chosen weapon, he revs it to life, its vicious teeth biting into the air. As the chainsaw roars, it tears through the attacking ghouls, splattering the area with gore and dismembered limbs.

The fast-food restaurant girl, Sally, crumples to the ground, her head taken clean off by a well-aimed shot from a security guard. Meanwhile, the bus driver and the basketball player zombie find themselves in the chainsaw-wielding assistant's merciless path. Relying on his past encounters, the assistant maneuvers the chainsaw with a ruthless accuracy, carving through the pair of zombies. The aftermath is a horrifying scene of dismembered bodies, torn and twisted beyond recognition, showcasing his efficient brutality.

These defenders, their faces etched with fear and exhaustion, hold the flanks with adrenaline-fueled ferocity. Each swing of their makeshift weapons illustrates their resolve. Despite the seemingly insurmountable odds, these survivors continue to fight, unwilling to surrender to the advancing walkers.

Behind the primary defense line, I notice civilians joining the fight, hurling bottles not directly at the approaching zombies but towards the ceiling. The bottles shatter on impact, and their liquid contents rain down upon the first line of zombies. To my surprise, it's not molotov cocktails, as there are no flaming rags in the bottles. Instead, it's a harsh, concentrated acid that starts to melt the skulls and bodies of the zombies as it splashes onto them. The strong, repugnant odor of decomposing flesh assaults my senses, causing an instinctive reaction of revulsion. The corrosive downpour takes out many of the attackers, their forms collapsing and dissolving into shocking, unrecognizable heaps on the ground, giving the defenders a much-needed advantage in their desperate battle.

The plaza is bathed in an eerie, flickering light from the damaged overhead fixtures, casting shadows that dance and twist across the blood-splattered floor. As I observe the scene, I realize that this is not the first battle these survivors have faced in the mall. There are other zombie corpses strewn along the corridor, and the surroundings bear the unmistakable signs of previous skirmishes, including older acid marks on the walls and floor. The clothing of many defenders is stained with dried blood, further evidence of their past encounters. Despite their makeshift weapons and ragtag appearance, the defenders seem to know what they're doing. They work together in perfect harmony, forming a highly effective fighting force against the unyielding swarm.

Yet, despite their valiant efforts, the horde continues its relentless advance, claiming more victims with each merciless step. The pizza delivery guy, momentarily lagging behind, is abruptly yanked into the ravenous mass by the muscular arm of the motorcyclist zombie, who emerges from the onslaught of the walking dead. Attempting to slice through the encroaching mass with his razor-sharp katana, the food court chef's weapon fails him. The cheaply made blade bends under the force, leaving him defenseless. As if on cue, the ghoul from the playground appears, lunging at him and sinking her teeth into his throat as he helplessly tries to fend her off. Another defender, a middle-aged man brandishing a makeshift spear, is blindsided by a zombie crawling unnoticed on the floor. The creature seizes his leg, dragging him down and begins to tear into his flesh. The grim reality of their dire situation becomes increasingly apparent as the survivors continue to battle the seemingly unstoppable tide of raging corpses.

In the midst of this nightmarish scene, the music in the headphone of the social warrior zombie shifts from Dies Irae to Domine Jesu, adding a hauntingly eerie soundtrack to the unfolding horror.

The survivors valiantly battle the walkers when a young man suddenly comes into view, sprinting through the chaos with reckless abandon. Wearing a dark hoodie and with an air of confidence about him, he holds his phone out in front of him, capturing a live video of the carnage as he narrates the events to his online audience.

"¡Hola, amigos! It's your boy, ThrillChaser, and as promised, I'm right here in the heart of the danger, giving you an exclusive look at this loco zombie outbreak!" He exclaims, his tone filled with adrenaline-fueled excitement. "You won't believe el caos happening here! I'm like, inches away from these terroríficas criaturas!"

As he leaps over a fallen display, he continues his commentary, "Nunca he visto algo así en mi vida, amigos. It's like a scene straight out of a horror movie. Estos zombies are relentless, and I'm right here in the thick of it!"

Some of the defenders momentarily glance at him, shouting, "Hey, get back here!" and "Have you lost your mind?" But the guy ignores the warnings, absorbed in his live broadcast.

It's a surreal sight, and I can't help but feel a mix of frustration and pity. Even in the face of death, some people are still willing to risk everything for a few more likes and followers.

The influencer deftly navigates the chaos, leaping over obstacles and dodging zombies with surprising agility. All the while, he excitedly narrates his daring escape to his online audience, who are no doubt glued to their screens, captivated by the harrowing scene that he's broadcasting live.

"So, for those of you just tuning in," he says breathlessly, "we've got a full-on zombie attack happening right here, en el centro comercial. The survivors are trying to hold their ground, and I'm giving you the most exclusive, up-close-and-personal look at the action! This is una locura, guys!"

He ducks beneath a swinging zombie arm and continues, "I don't know how much longer these brave people can hold out, but I'm aquí to show you what's really going on, no matter the risk!" In his eyes, I can see that he made a bad call and is just realizing it.

He pauses to catch his breath, then adds with a grin, "Don't forget to smash that like button and share this stream with your amigos! This is the kind of content you won't find anywhere else, ¡es una locura!" he exclaims, moments before his luck runs out. He misjudges a leap and tumbles to the ground, immediately swarmed by the ravenous horde. His screams pierce the air, filled with terror and agony as he is devoured before his adoring audience.

As I pass by the scene of his grisly demise, I notice his phone lying on the ground, still broadcasting the live video. For a brief moment, I catch a glimpse of the comments on the screen.

One follower writes, "OMG, I can't believe he's gone! :'(" while another coldly quips, "Well, that's one way to go viral." Another comment reads, "He got what he deserved, playing with danger like that. Smh -_-" Yet another chimes in with, "RIP, Diego. Your vids were sick, but this was just too much. Hasta siempre, amigo."

These comments highlight the fickle nature of the influencer's audience, a mix of shock, sympathy, and disdain, all vying for attention. It's a morbid testament to the depths of human folly and our obsession with fleeting fame, even as the world falls apart around us.

As the abominations unceasingly pursue the survivors through the mall's labyrinthine corridors, the chilling melody of Domine Jesu reverberates through the night, a haunting dirge that underscores the darkness that has befallen us. As the chaos unfolds before me, I'm gripped by curiosity about the strange selection process that determines who is merely consumed and who joins the ranks of the monsters. I watch the creatures, noticing their instinctual, predatory behavior. Their movements are swift, decisive, and single-minded.

An unsettling thought takes root: perhaps the virus isn't haphazard in its choice of host but is drawn to specific traits discerned through scent. It could seek out individuals with genetic or physiological characteristics that make them more compatible with the infection. This might explain why some people are transformed while others serve as sustenance. The disease could be hunting suitable hosts to perpetuate its existence, much like a parasite.

As the defenders engage in their desperate, losing battle, they yell encouragements to one another and the frightened civilians: "Keep moving! Don't stop! We'll cover you!" Their voices, filled with steadfastness and courage, reverberate through the bloodsplattered mall. I witness the shop assistant's chainsaw roar to life over and over again, its teeth viciously tearing through the monstrous flesh, sending sprays of dark blood and chunks of rotten meat flying. The gruesome scene unfolds like a nightmarish ballet, with the chainsaw's thunderous roar providing a disturbing soundtrack.

Despite the odds, the formidable defenders gradually thin the ranks of the terrifying legion ahead of me. As the constant surge of my infected brethren carries me forward, I find myself inexorably drawn nearer to the frontline - and the lethal whirl of the chainsaw. Meanwhile, the security guards manage to take down a few more creatures with precise headshots, reloading their weapons with impressive speed. It seems they have no shortage of ammunition, likely scavenged from somewhere within the mall.

The music in the social justice warrior zombie's headphones shifts from Dies Irae to Lacrymosa. I find it ironic that this zombie is listening to Requiem, the final work of Wolfgang Amadeus Mozart's life. Sarah had taught me about Requiem, as it was one of her favorites, along with Vivaldi's Four Seasons. It's a haunting, yet fitting soundtrack to the chaos around me.

A tall security guard with a commanding presence, Bennett, as indicated by the name on his uniform, starts to issue orders to the other defenders as they back into a narrow corridor. "Everyone, fall back! Shepherd the new survivors back to the fort!" His voice, steady and authoritative, cuts through the chaos. It's becoming clear to me that this group of survivors was on a mission to rescue others when they presumably bumped into this horde, forcing them to fight their way back to the safety of their fortification.

The Praetorian cosplayer, acknowledging Bennett's orders, barks out commands to the two legionnaires beside him, using Roman phrases and terminology. "Legionarii, tenete positionem! Formate testudinem!" I remember some Latin from my school days and private diligence, and I translate the orders to myself as I hear them: "Legionnaires, hold your position! Tortoise formation!" The legionnaires respond with discipline, holding the line in the

Roman style as they prepare to cover the retreat of their fellow defenders.

The three Roman soldiers span the width of the narrow corridor with their scutum shields, meticulously retreating while maintaining their defensive formation. It becomes evident to me that their retreat is purposeful. Rallying around Bennett, the survivors follow his lead back through the corridor. The hot-dog retailer, fitness instructor, nurse, and other battle-weary and exhausted survivors join the security guards, forming a protective barrier behind the cosplayers.

As I watch the swarm arrive at the choke point, I find myself in about the fifteenth row of zombies in the narrow corridor as the mass of creatures piles up. I can't help but suspect that the defenders might actually be driving the swarm into a trap, considering their impressive level of organization. The thought of what could possibly await us at the "fort" where the survivors retreat fills me with unease and dread, but I'm powerless to do anything other than follow the tide of the walkers.

The legionnaires, with their gladius swords at the ready, skillfully thrust through the heads of the advancing zombies, efficiently taking them down one by one. The Praetorian Centurion, commanding and battle-hardened, raises his voice, shouting encouragement and tactical advice to his fellow legionnaires in Latin: "Firmate animos! Pugnate pro vobis et pro amicis!" As he shouts, I recall a little more Latin from my school days and translate his words in my head: "Be strong! Fight for yourselves and for your friends!"

In a fleeting moment, I manage to catch a glimpse of the Praetorian's face. Despite the grim situation, he exudes a sense of enjoyment, seeming to relish the heat of the battle. His eyes blaze with fierce determination and an almost fanatical zeal, suggesting he'd always dreamed of embodying the heroic figure he now portrays. This man, who appears to be in his early thirties and likely still living in his parents' basement, is fully embracing the opportunity to live out his fantasy amidst the chaos. The real-world apocalypse has afforded him the unexpected role of a lifetime, and he's seized it with both hands.

The defenders reach the end of the narrow corridor, which leads through large metal doors, presumably to the cargo bay of the mall. As the zombies, myself included, march forward, I notice a makeshift misting station rigged above us. Pieced together from various hardware store components, it hangs ominously overhead, awaiting activation.

As the backing legionnaires and the praetorian pass underneath it, the station comes to life with a sudden hiss, dousing the advancing zombies in a fine spray of liquid. The droplets glisten as they cling to our undead bodies, forming a wet sheen on our skin and clothes.

The pungent smell of rubbing alcohol fills the air, instantly alerting me to the trap that has been set. A surge of desperation floods my mind as I wish to flee, but my body refuses to obey, continuing its unceasing pursuit of the living despite the imminent danger. The misting station continues to douse us in the flammable liquid, ensuring that we are thoroughly soaked and primed for the coming inferno.

Upon ensuring the survivors have crossed the threshold of the metal doors, a legionnaire bellows, "Now!" Almost in response,

Molotov cocktails arc over the Roman defenders and land amid the vanguard of the zombie horde. The glass containers shatter on impact, cloaking the infected in an immediate blaze. In seamless coordination, the legionnaires and Praetorian raise their scutums, the large shields deflecting the heat and protecting both themselves and the survivors behind them.

With the zombies engulfed in flames and temporarily halted, the Roman warriors leverage this moment to their advantage. Pressing their shields forward, they thrust back against the burning ghouls, their combined strength propelling the infected away from the doorway and deeper into the fiery onslaught. Overwhelmed and unable to resist, the zombies are driven back into the inferno's belly, where the flames continue their relentless consumption.

The Praetorian then shouts out a command in Latin, "Recipite! Conclude portas!" I quickly translate this in my head: "Retreat! Lock the doors!"

Using the momentum of their swift and decisive actions, the survivors escape through the metal doors, and the fireproof barrier slams shut behind them, effectively sealing off the burning horde. I watch helplessly as the fire spreads across the alcohol-soaked zombies, and soon, I too am engulfed in the searing flames.

5

The pain is excruciating as the flames lick at my undead flesh, charring and blackening the skin. I can almost feel the virus writhing within me as if it, too, is tormented by the scorching heat. My body collapses to the ground, the agonizing sensation overwhelming even the insatiable hunger that drives the ravenous horde.

Just as the pain seems unbearable, the mall's water sprinkler fire suppression system suddenly activates. Powerful jets of water rain down from the ceiling, dousing the fire and soaking the burning zombies, including myself. The water creates a cooling barrier that effectively extinguishes the flames.

The other zombies lie motionless on the ground around me, drenched and smoldering. For a moment, I believe I might be the only one who survived the encounter. However, as I continue to observe my surroundings, I notice the other zombies begin to stir once more, their movements slight at first.

As they regain their bearings, I realize that the rubbing alcohol must have burned at a lower temperature, which merely scorched our clothes and left us relatively unharmed. The few zombies who were directly hit by the Molotov cocktails do not move again –

their bodies are burnt beyond recognition, an indication of the devastating power of the improvised weapons.

It becomes clear that the survivors are not fools. They must have deliberately kept the fire suppression system on to avoid burning down the entire mall that provides them refuge. This realization only reinforces the fact that the living will go to great lengths to survive. Furthermore, I suspect that the use of alcohol instead of gasoline for the trap is a result of the survivors managing their limited resources. It seems that gasoline is more scarce in their inventory than alcohol, so they use it sparingly and only in situations where its effectiveness is crucial, like in the Molotov cocktails.

In the aftermath of the intense trauma from the fire, I sense that something within my body has shifted in a way that I can't quite explain. It's as if the contagion inside me has adapted in response to the ordeal, but the true extent of these changes remains a mystery.

Every movement my body makes causes intense pain. I would scream if I could, but all that leaves my lips is an angry growl. Despite the searing pain, I continue to move, driven by the hunger that plagues me. My consciousness barely hangs on, nearly overwhelmed by the indescribable pain that threatens to consume me. Then, suddenly, the pain starts to ease as if my body begins to heal itself.

Gradually, my charred and cracked skin begins to peel away, revealing a fresh layer underneath. This raw, exposed flesh swiftly adopts a healthier hue, as if untouched by fire. With each passing moment, my skin self-mends, growing smoother and more uniform.

Catching my reflection in a puddle on the floor, I notice something unexpected - my hair, previously singed away, is regrowing, returning to its original length and color.

The pathogen within me proves not only capable of hijacking its host's body like a ruthless parasite, taking total control, but it also possesses an incredible ability to regenerate and repair damaged tissues. This discovery holds both fascinating and horrifying implications, suggesting that the infected may be even harder to kill than previously thought.

The eerie transformation isn't unique to me, however. All the zombies incinerated in the corridor are experiencing the same resurrection. Some, like the motorcyclist, the little girl, and others who've suffered severe damage, endure an unnerving transformation. Their human forms twist and shudder in sync with the infection's rhythm coursing through their veins. It's as if the virus is conducting a grotesque symphony of internal restructuring beneath their skin, propelling them towards a horrific evolution that promises an even greater threat.

Slowly, the blackened zombies rise, their bodies still smoldering from the fiery ordeal. Despite the substantial damage, the relentless pathogen drives them to resume their pursuit of the living. The social justice warrior zombie, her partially melted headphones stubbornly clinging to her head, stands out. From the ruined speakers, distorted music seeps out, adding an uncanny melody to our chilling tableau. I strain to recognize the tune, but the damage renders it unidentifiable.

As my body rises along with them, it immediately turns toward the closed fireproof door. Two zombies approach the sturdy metal barrier that separates them from the survivors. They cautiously raise their arms and begin to tap and scratch at the door, testing its strength. Their movements are slow and deliberate, as if they're trying to find a weakness in the door's construction. Frustrated growls emanate from their throats as they come to the realization that they won't be getting through here.

Their growls catch the attention of the rest of the undead mass. One by one, the zombies, including myself, turn around to face the direction from which they came. It's as if they've collectively understood that their prey has escaped, and there's no use in trying to break through the door. Their focus shifts, and they begin to wander away, searching for other victims to satisfy their unending cravings. The horde assembles, driven by the unyielding hunger that fuels us. As we venture further, we catch the scent of new prey, and the swarm moves in unison towards the source.

The survivor's fierce and strategic defense has whittled our numbers down considerably, leaving only about twenty of us. This grim reduction sparks a frail flame of hope within me. I can't help but contemplate the potential that, with our diminished ranks, the nightmarish cycle could be nearing its end. Perhaps, in this dire circumstance, there lies the chance for every tormented soul here to find their long-awaited peace.

As our hideous appearance belies the cold and cunning precision with which the contagion guides its reanimated hosts, I can't help but ponder the true purpose of this unyielding force. The realization that an intelligent pathogen is controlling our every move fills me with a deep sense of dread, even in my ghastly state. What could be the end goal of this seemingly unstoppable plague?

Emerging from the scorched corridor back into the main thoroughfare of the mall, we encounter a zombie shuffling past. The young man's shirt proudly proclaims, "Eat Green, Live Clean: Proud to be Vegetarian!" The sentiment now provides a striking contrast to his macabre pursuit for human flesh.

My attention then shifts to the old lady with the gardening tool, who had previously been engulfed in our eerie collective. Recently, however, she moved away from me, staying just out of sight.

Now, as she comes into focus, it becomes apparent that there's something unique about her. Despite her beastly snarls, her mouth remains devoid of blood, as if her body, much like mine, has refrained from attacking the living. Her overall demeanor sets her apart from the others, and as I scrutinize her further, I can see a subtle flicker of emotion and disorientation lurking behind the cursed orange glow of her eyes. Her eyes dart around wildly, appearing desperate and on the brink of insanity, as if she wants to scream with every fiber of her being but can't.

Struck by an inexplicable impulse, I attempt to communicate. A rough growl rumbles in my chest, emerging as an unintelligible garble. To my surprise, she answers. Her response is equally primal, a series of hauntingly familiar growls. It's a bizarre conversation, void of any real language, yet it conveys a raw, desperate connection.

The realization that she might also be caught within her own reanimated form, fighting against the iron grasp of the infection, creeps up on me. This common struggle against our horrific existence silently binds us, offering a shred of comfort amid the turmoil.

Unveiling such a startling truth fills me with both dread and intrigue. It paves the way for countless questions about the nature of the virus and the depth of its control over its victims. How many in the crowd might still be clutching onto some level of awareness, perpetually wrestling with the infection? Most critically, could there be a way for us to seize back control and put an end to this terrifying nightmare? The dim light throws unnerving shadows on the faces of the cursed, heightening the somber mood as I grapple with the enormity of these inquiries.

As we continue moving, my eyes fall on three zombies in the front lines, way ahead of me. They break into the mall's pet shop, and a heart-wrenching sight awaits me inside. One zombie is ravaging the parrots, their once vibrant, colorful feathers now stained with gore as they screech in pain and terror. My gaze then falls upon a small white poodle, its once-pristine fur now soaked in blood. The dog has been bitten and transformed into a monstrous version of itself, a blood poodle, snarling and snapping at anything that comes too close.

The horde continues its way through the mall, eventually reaching the locked and chained glass doors. For a short time, the gates withstand their efforts, but then some of the morphed zombies, including the motorcyclist guy and Bob the service guy, unleash their newfound strength. They tear the doors open, shattering the glass and breaking the metal chains that once stood as a barrier between them and their prey. The horde spills back into the city, intent on claiming more victims and swelling their ranks.

As I follow the ravenous horde back into the city, I can't help but hope that our significantly reduced numbers will make it easier for the defenders to finally put an end to this nightmare. With fewer of us left to contend with, perhaps the living can swiftly eradicate the remaining zombies, allowing everyone, both living and infected, to finally find some semblance of peace.

Overhead, helicopters buzz through the smoke-filled skies. Some appear to be evacuating survivors, lifting them to safety from the rooftops, while another, a police helicopter, hovers nearby. Inside, two passengers - one spotter and one sniper - scan the area for threats. The sniper takes aim and swiftly eliminates two zombies from my pack with two precise shots.

As the small horde persistently forges ahead, the city's atmosphere grows more oppressive and tense. Shadows dance and flicker under the sickly yellow glow of the streetlights, casting an eerie pall over the once bustling streets. Up ahead, about two blocks away, red and blue lights flash in the darkness, as a line of police cars forms a makeshift barricade. Behind them, a large number of survivors stand at the ready—brave police officers from various districts armed with shotguns, SWAT members with riot shields, and desperate civilians wielding rifles and pistols. They prepare for the imminent clash, loading their guns and taking aim at the approaching undead menace. Others clutch makeshift Molotov cocktails, waiting for the right moment to hurl them with reckless abandon in a frantic effort to repel the advancing throng.

The sniper in the helicopter takes aim once more, eliminating the vegetarian zombie in front of me with a single, well-placed shot. Despite the grim situation, I can't help but think that at least the vegetarian zombie stayed true to his ideals, never tasting meat in this new life. Realizing I'm likely the next target, I begin to mentally prepare myself for the end. Clasping onto every fragment of my past life, the memories that tether me to sanity, I find my refuge, my beacon in this nightmare. I recall smiles, laughter, love - echoes of a life now lost but never forgotten. The hope that the end will be swift and merciful offers me a small measure of comfort.

However, just as I steel myself for the inevitable, the spotter in the helicopter points towards a nearby street, and the helicopter suddenly veers away to investigate. As the helicopter's searchlight sweeps towards the indicated area, a deep, rumbling growl echoes through the air, growing louder and more menacing with each passing second. The sound doesn't seem to be coming from my cluster, but from the direction the helicopter is now focused on.

As the sniper quickly reloads, he starts taking shots at whatever threat the helicopter is now targeting. His actions are methodical and precise, each shot fired in rapid succession with great professionalism. Although I can't see what he's shooting at, it's clear that the sniper is taking down more than ten targets in a matter of seconds, displaying remarkable skill and efficiency.

As we reach the intersection, just one block away from the defenders' barricades, a large truck barrels into view, steering too fast as it smashes through a few zombies from my group. The vehicle's momentum sends the creatures flying, their bodies crushed and mangled under the truck's massive wheels. Losing control, the truck skids sideways on the slick pavement, grinding to a halt with a screech of tortured metal. Behind the truck, a massive horde of zombies appears from around the corner, numbering well over a half thousand.

As the ravenous multitude converges, I find myself engulfed within the unnerving symphony of their growls and snarls. Among the new recruits, a disheveled taxi driver, his once neat turban now wild and tattered, stands out. Nearby, Dave, a shopkeeper whose dark skin is now obscured by the chaos of the outbreak, is hardly recognizable. His apron is smeared with gore, and his previously friendly demeanor has been replaced by a chilling hunger. A gaunt banker in a ruined suit shuffles alongside a once captivating striptease dancer, her allure replaced with repulsive sores. Lastly, a dustman's robust form is twisted, his reflective vest tattered. Amid these horrors, I spot several mutated abominations, their twisted limbs and exaggerated features a stark display of the virus's monstrous creativity.

The driver attempts a desperate escape from the wreckage of the truck, his eyes brimming with terror. Yet, he quickly falls prey to the relentless walkers, his demise underscoring the human cost of this apocalyptic nightmare. Then, in an act of mercy, a sharp crack echoes from above—the report of a sniper rifle. The driver's struggle abruptly ends, taken out by the sniper in the helicopter that's been circling overhead.

As I witness the scene unfolding before me, I understand that the nightmare is far from over. Instead of a swift end, the defenders now face an even more formidable and overwhelming force, as the zombie hordes unite and press onward, driven by an insatiable hunger for human flesh. This disturbing display of intelligent coordination only serves to confirm my suspicions that there is a sinister and calculated force at work behind the virus's actions. I can see the shock on the defenders' faces, their determination now replaced by a mixture of shock and fear, as they realize they are overwhelmed by the sheer number of the attacking ghouls. With the zombie masses merging, the police helicopter circles back, strafing between the defenders and the advancing swarm. It flies low, whipping up the air with its rotor and creating a disorienting gust. As the helicopter turns, its searchlight sweeps across the rooftops, instantly drawing my attention. That's when I notice five tiny, shiny objects glinting in the light, each placed not far from the others. The realization dawns on me - they're sniper scopes.

Bullets tear through the air, leaving trails of acrid smoke in their wake as they find their targets within the undead flood. Among the rooftop snipers, I recognize Jackson, the SWAT commander, his eyes focused and steely as he expertly takes down several zombies in a synchronized attack with the other sharpshooters But despite their efforts, the advance of the horde continues, an unstoppable tide of decay and hunger surging ever closer to the desperate and determined defenders.

As we draw nearer, the tension among the defenders is evident. One of the police officers, a seasoned sergeant with a steely gaze, raises his hand and barks out an order: "Open fire! Make every shot count!" The survivors brace themselves, aiming for the heads of the advancing zombies, as they prepare to unleash a hail of bullets and fire upon the approaching swarm. A symphony of gunfire fills the air, punctuated by the staccato rhythm of spent shell casings clattering to the ground.

I catch sight of Jackson, his eyes widen in shock, and I'm certain I see his lips form the words, "I'm sorry, Steve." Just as he pulls the trigger, my body instinctively begins to strafe rapidly, evading the oncoming bullets as if it knows from my memories the threat Jackson represents. Jackson's surprise is evident on his face, and he is determined to land a hit on me, no matter the cost. He ejects the spent cartridge and swiftly loads the next one into the sniper rifle before firing again. The shots miss me, but I hear the impact as they strike other zombies behind me.

The unexpected responsiveness of my body leaves me stunned. It's as if the virus controlling my actions possesses a level of intelligence, not just predatory instincts. The realization is both fascinating and deeply unsettling, making me question the true nature of the force that has taken over my body.

The sound of bullets slicing through the air is deafening, my heightened senses acutely aware of each lethal projectile as it narrowly misses my head. A surge of primal alertness courses through me, a brutal reminder of the deadly threat at hand amidst the unrelenting chaos.

However, the mutated zombies seem to thrive on the chaos and destruction, their bodies adapting and growing stronger with each injury inflicted upon them. Their grotesque forms become more monstrous and fearsome with every passing moment, a vivid demonstration of the insidious power of the infection coursing through their veins.

As the battle rages on around me, I witness the bright flash of molotov cocktails exploding nearby, their fiery bursts engulfing several unfortunate zombies in a searing blaze. The scent of burning flesh mixes with the discord of chaos, intensifying the nightmarish scene. Screams of agony from the burning undead pierce the air, adding to the sense of despair and terror.

Suddenly, I feel a sharp, searing pain in my body as the one of the bullets from Jackson finds its mark. My enhanced reflexes and heightened senses betray me, amplifying the sensation of the impact. I can feel the hot metal tearing through my flesh, my muscles tensing with the hit. Panic and fear threaten to overwhelm me, but a flicker of tenacity remains—a stubborn refusal to succumb to the monstrous forces that have consumed so many others.

My body undergoes a transformation in response to the trauma, as if tapping into a hidden reserve of strength. An electrifying surge of power courses through my ravaged veins, redefining the limits of my physical abilities. I sense the change within me as my body becomes more tenacious, more robust, and more agile, ready to face the challenges ahead.

As Jackson reloads again, he aims and fires with determination, but my body evades once more. In the reflection of a nearby window, I witness another zombie receiving a headshot behind me—it's the social justice warrior girl. Her body crumples to the ground, her brightly-colored headphones clattering to the pavement beside her, tearing down some part of her melted skin as they fall. The haunting silence that follows is broken only by the soft, melancholic melody that continues to play from the abandoned headphones, a stark contrast to the discord of death and destruction that surrounds us.

The ceaseless battle continues around me. The motorcyclist's arm transforms into a massive, bony shield, and like an unstoppable juggernaut, he crashes through the barricade. The little girl, now endowed with razor-sharp claws and incredible speed, emits a spine-chilling, high-pitched scream as she darts through the opening. Her relentless assault leaves a gruesome trail of blood and carnage in her wake, tearing through the beleaguered defenders with terrifying ease. In the midst of his horrific transformation, the service guy Bob becomes the target of a desperate counterattack. An improvised molotov cocktail, thrown by a terrified survivor, arcs through the air and collides with his grotesque form. The glass shatters upon impact, dousing his twisted body in flames.

The fire rages, consuming his monstrous tentacles as they writhe and contort in a sickening dance of agony. The putrid smell of burning flesh fills the air, mingling with the sounds of battle and the horrified screams of the living. As Bob's shrieks of torment pierce the tumultuous din, the flames voraciously devour his ghoulish flesh, reducing his once-human form to a smoldering, unrecognizable husk.

Despite the gruesome sight, the remaining survivors cling to this small, fleeting victory, a brief respite from the nightmarish tide of undead that continues to bear down upon them. Their faces, etched with fear and steadfastness, stand as a bold display of their unwavering resolve to fight on in the face of unspeakable horror.

The police helicopter hovers behind the defenders and the sniper quickly reloads, a mutated zombie suddenly emerges from the horde, its repulsive form twisted beyond recognition. Its back is covered in sharp spines, each about 30 centimeters in length. With a guttural snarl, it arches its back, launching a volley of deadly projectiles into the air.

The lethal spines rain down upon the police helicopter, catching the sniper and spotter off guard and impaling them with sickening precision. One spine even crashes through the window, skewering the pilot in an instant. The helicopter, now bereft of control, begins to spin wildly, its rotors slicing through the air as it veers off course. With a deafening explosion, the doomed aircraft crashes into a nearby house, erupting into a fireball that casts an ominous glow over the surrounding chaos.

The helicopter's explosion illuminates the area, revealing another zombie lurking in the shadows. I recognize the bloodstained apron and tattered chef's hat, suggesting it had once worked in the luxury restaurant the horde had attacked. The zombie displays an unnerving agility, moving like a skilled mountain climber. With a terrifying grace, it clambers up the side of a building, using its unnaturally elongated claws to cling to the facade. Its former hobby as a mountain climber seems to have been twisted and repurposed by the virus, providing it with a deadly advantage in its monstrous form.

The unsuspecting snipers perched on the rooftops, focused on picking off the advancing undead below, remain oblivious to the approaching threat. The mutated zombie closes in on them, its ghastly form a twisted shadow against the building's exterior. As it reaches the rooftop, it lunges at the nearest sniper, its claws slashing through the air in a deadly arc. The rooftop erupts into chaos, as the remaining snipers scramble to defend themselves against this unexpected and terrifying foe. Amidst the confusion, I hear Jackson's voice, barking out an order: "Fall back! Everyone, retreat now!" The fate of Jackson and his fellow snipers remains uncertain as my view is obscured by the buildings and the ever-growing legion of walkers.

In the midst of the chaos, the disoriented elderly woman, who appeared to be struggling to maintain her consciousness within her reanimated form, is struck by a bullet to the head close to me and falls lifelessly to the ground. I feel a pang of sorrow for her, but perhaps death is a release from the torment she was experiencing.

As she collapses, I notice a medical ID bracelet on her wrist. On the bracelet, I can see her name – Edith Collins, a mention of Alzheimer's disease, a partially obscured emergency contact phone number. The additional details on the bracelet suggest that she might have been a member of a support group or an organization related to her condition. Finally her blood type: AB+, the same as mine.

My mind flashes back to a conversation with my academy classmate, Sato, while we were studying in our dorm room. He was preparing for an upcoming medical exam and asked me to quiz him on blood transfusions. I realized that I didn't know much about my own blood type, which I had only discovered when I applied to the academy, as I never had much of an injury as a child or a teenager, aside from a few broken bones here and there. Wanting to learn more, I asked, "What can you tell me about AB+ blood type?"

Sato replied, "Oh, that's the 'universal recipient.' AB+ can receive blood from any other type, but can only donate to others with AB+ blood. In fact, only about 3% of the population has this blood type." I try to picture his face, but it remains a blur, just like the surreal nightmares that haunt me.

Surprised, I responded, "Really? That's quite rare indeed. Well, it turns out I'm part of that small percentage – AB+ is my blood type."

"Lucky you! You won't have to wait in line for a transfusion if needed," Sato said with a smile.

"Hopefully, I won't ever need one," I remarked, unaware that I would be shot during my first year of service, and receiving a blood transfusion would save my life.

Sato continued, "In Japan, we have this Ketsueki-Gata theory, which is a popular belief that a person's blood type can determine their personality traits. According to this theory, AB+ individuals are considered to be adaptable, diplomatic, rational, and patient. It's not scientifically proven, of course, but it's an interesting cultural perspective. You certainly appear to exhibit those qualities, my friend."

I chuckled, "Well, lucky me then, having those traits attributed to my blood type. Maybe they'll come in handy someday."

Sato smiled, "Just remember, it's more of a cultural belief than a scientific fact. But I must say, I've witnessed your adaptability and diplomacy in action, like the time you skillfully resolved the conflict between Callahan and Delgado in the academy dining hall."

Reflecting on the current predicament, the role of blood type in this infection surfaces in my mind. I envision the pathogen, swift and relentless, invading blood cells, and altering healthy ones with destructive enzymes and toxins. The rapid transformation post-bite could be the contagion acclimatizing to its host, reaching its destructive peak within minutes.

Drawing on Sato's insights on blood types, it appears blood type could be a determinant in the spread of infection. Universal donors like O-, and others like A+, A-, B+, B-, AB-, and O+ can propagate the contagion, but as an AB+ individual, I can't easily pass it on.

Interestingly, my AB+ blood cells appear to adapt and resist the pathogen rather than easily surrendering. This resistance, rooted in the unique antigens of my blood type, may hinder the virus from taking full control and explain my restrained urge to attack others. My consciousness remains active, potentially due to the virus's struggle to breach the blood-brain barrier in AB+ individuals. This creates a delicate balance: while the pathogen drives a persistent hunger for other blood types, my consciousness holds it in check, maintaining an unlikely control over the infection's urges.

My theory suggests that the virus uses bites for reproduction, much like a tick fortifies itself by feeding and spreading disease. This need for reproduction, possibly tied to the donor-recipient relationship, could drive the infected's intense hunger to infect or consume others. Should this theory prove accurate, the interaction between my blood type and the virus may be crucial to my semi-resistance and preserved consciousness.

While I ponder on these theories, the legion continues to press forward, slowly but surely overwhelming the remaining defenders. Their desperate efforts to hold the line seem to be in vain. As I watch the scene unfold before me, I am beset with inner turmoil. The coordinated assault appears almost strategic, as if the infection itself were orchestrating the movements of its monstrous minions.

The haunting realization that the infection might possess a malevolent intelligence only serves to heighten my despair and fuels my desperate struggle to resist its insidious control.

The carnage eventually comes to an end and the mass of zombies treads on, yet my body inexplicably halts its advance. To my surprise, I find myself slowly drifting away from the group. Something within me has shifted, as if a subtle force has pulled me back from the brink of losing myself entirely to the infection.

As I stand bewildered, the first drops of rain begin to fall, casting a somber veil over the gruesome scene. The rainfall grows steadily heavier, its persistent patter creating an eerie soundtrack to the unfolding apocalypse. Puddles form on the cracked pavement, their dark surfaces reflecting the storm-laden skies above. It's as if the rain is attempting to wash away the blood staining the streets. The horde continues to move forward without me; my mind races, attempting to decipher this unexpected shift. Why am I no longer driven to follow the others? Is it possible that my will has regained some control over my zombified body? The prospect of escaping this nightmare stirs a turbulent mix of hope and fear within me. I'm left to wonder about the road ahead and whether I can truly resist the relentless grasp of the infection.

Despite my yearning for the oblivion of sleep, it remains elusive. My eyes are wide open; I am an eternal insomniac in the darkness of the night, a state that only heightens my sense of isolation. The lingering scents of blood and fire blend with the damp, earthy aroma of the rain-soaked city, forming a sensory collage as disconcerting as it is captivating. This mixture of scents, reminiscent of fresh praline, vanilla, black currants, pear, and the undertones of freshly tilled soil and petrichor, lingers hauntingly in the air.

Drawn in by the familiar yet elusive fragrance, my virus-controlled body navigates the dim, rain-soaked backstreets of the city, once vibrant but now filled with dread. The scent calls to me, much like a siren's enchanting melody, invigorating my senses in a manner that awakens the primal predator within me. Letting out a deep, primal growl—a response that even I struggle to comprehend—I find myself succumbing to a compelling impulse. Breaking into an assertive sprint, I relentlessly pursue the tantalizing scent that hovers at the periphery of my consciousness.

The sound of my own footfalls echo in my ears, each step a hollow drumbeat against the silence. It's a rhythm that belies the frenzy in my veins, a grim soundtrack to my nightmarish reality. As my virus-controlled body navigates the shadowy, rain-drenched alley, the clamor of another skirmish escalates in the vicinity. The sharp crack of gunshots and terrified cries ripple through the air, signifying a desperate last stand by survivors against the ceaseless tide of the undead. The rain persists in its heavy downpour, punctuated by sporadic flashes of lightning that fleetingly light up the murky gloom, succeeded by the resonating rumble of thunder echoing across the cityscape.

As I emerge into a spacious square, a startling sight greets me: a small band of soldiers and terrified civilians facing an onslaught of about thirty zombies. Once a bustling hub, the square has transformed into a nightmarish battleground, its cobblestone streets slick with rain and blood. The soldiers, soaked to the bone, their uniforms clinging to their bodies, fight with grim determination. Occasional flashes from discharged weapons sporadically illuminate their fatigue-stricken faces. Amidst the chaos, a commanding cry of a soldier echoes, "Hold the line! We can't let them get through!"

They unleash a thunderous symphony of gunfire in an attempt to repel the tireless onslaught of the ghoulish invaders. The civilians huddle together behind makeshift barriers, cowering in the pouring rain. Their eyes, wide with terror, dart frantically from one horrifying scene to another as they cling to one another for comfort and support.

The torrential downpour casts a bleak, oppressive atmosphere over the scene, as lightning streaks across the sky, illuminating the chaotic battle in stark flashes. The rumble of thunder mixes with the ceaseless gunfire and guttural moans of the undead, creating an eerie symphony of destruction. Puddles of rainwater and gore collect on the ground, reflecting the hellish scene above in distorted, swirling patterns. As the last line of defense, the soldiers hold their ground, their eyes filled with a steely resolve, even as the odds seem insurmountable. A soldier yells to his comrades, "Keep firing!"

The soldiers and zombies clash in a brutal dance of life and death. With every passing moment, the line between the two sides threatens to break, casting a shadow of uncertainty over the fate of the remaining survivors. Despite my own monstrous form, an inexplicable urge to help these people begins to stir within me, though I know they would likely see me as an enemy rather than an ally.

Among the survivors, I spot the familiar face of Sarah, shielded by a fireman I've frequently encountered at various scenes within our district. His name eludes me, yet his distinctive features stand out - the deep richness of his skin, a beard carefully groomed to frame his face, and a weathered countenance bearing the signs of age and experience. This man, always ready to defuse tension with a well-timed joke, is a seasoned veteran of his trade, a beacon of calm professionalism amidst the chaos. Rain drenches his determined face and soaks his jacket as he wields his fire axe with deadly precision, cutting down any zombie daring to approach Sarah. "Stay behind me! I'll keep you safe!" His words ring out over the chaos, an affirmation of his unwavering courage and fierce protectiveness, providing a glimmer of hope amidst the turmoil.

The soldiers work in unison, quickly reloading, aiming, and firing their weapons with deadly precision. Their coordination and skill manage to thin the horde, each shot finding its mark in the head of a shambling zombie. As time passes, the soldiers maintain their focus and determination, until finally, the last zombie falls.

The civilians, now breathing a collective sigh of relief, express their gratitude to the soldiers. "Thank you so much!" one woman exclaims, tears streaming down her face. "You saved our lives," adds an older man, his voice shaking with emotion.

As everyone starts to regain their composure, the commander of the squad, a stern, middle-aged man with short-cropped hair and a steely gaze, suddenly raises his hand. "Hold your positions," he orders, his voice cold and authoritative. "Eliminate them all." The ominous command cuts through the air, casting a shadow of dread over the survivors who moments ago were filled with relief and gratitude.

The deafening sound of gunfire erupts as the soldiers open fire on the defenseless civilians. Screams of terror are drowned out by the unending barrage of bullets. The once hopeful survivors, now betrayed by those they perceived as protectors, crumple to the ground as bullets tear through their bodies.

A young mother clutches her infant child tightly, a futile attempt to shield the little one from the ruthless onslaught, only to be cut down in a hail of gunfire. Nearby, an elderly man, moments ago attempting to comfort his terrified wife, collapses onto her lifeless form, his face a mask of raw anguish. A teenage boy, his eyes wide with horror, tries to run but is swiftly mowed down, his body crumpling in a grotesque dance of death. A couple, holding onto each other in their final moments, fall together, their entwined bodies a poignant testament to their shared fate. A man in his thirties, perhaps a father or a husband, who had tried to reason with the soldiers, falls down, his pleas cut short. One by one, the civilians fall to the unforgiving, rain-soaked ground, their life essence seeping out to mingle with the bitter rain.

As I approach the heart of the conflict, a remarkable transformation takes place within my body. The line between my zombie form and human consciousness blurs, as my willpower seizes control. Large, razor-sharp bone claws extend from my hands, shimmering menacingly in the pale moonlight. I emerge from the shadows, my consciousness rebelling against the pathogen's control, fueled by the desire to save Sarah and the remaining civilians from the merciless execution. Rain pours down, creating an atmosphere of tension and despair as the soldiers continue their unceasing assault, cutting down one civilian after another. My heart aches for the innocent lives being taken, and with each step closer, my resolve to resist the infection and intervene intensifies.

I break into a sprint, my mind racing to find a way to save Sarah and the survivors. The urgency of the situation weighs heavily on me as I prepare to make my move, knowing I may only have one opportunity to make a difference. The fate of Sarah and the others hangs in the balance, and it's up to me to change the course of this nightmare. The sound of gunfire and terrified screams fills the air, further heightening the tension and sense of urgency.

As the lightning above illuminates the battleground in a flash of eerie light, casting an otherworldly glow on my fearsome form, one of the soldiers notices me. His eyes widen in fear. Fueled by desperation, he manages to steady his aim and opens fire on me. The bullets tear through my infected body, leaving a trail of gore in their wake. However, to the soldier's horror, the wounds do little to hinder my relentless advance. My body, driven by the insidious infection coursing through my veins, seems impervious to the pain that would have incapacitated me in my previous life.

Approaching the first soldier, I take note of his youth; he appears barely out of his teens. Despite his tender years, he has been drilled into mindless obedience, ready to massacre innocent civilians at a command. Yet, there is no pity stirring within me. The moment these soldiers chose to aim their weapons at the helpless, they determined their own grim destiny.

Swiftly obliterating the gap between us, I surge forward, propelled by an unearthly strength. My limbs coil and spring, catapulting me into the air. The young soldier, barely having the time to react, raises his rifle in a last-ditch attempt to protect himself. But his efforts are futile. With a swift swipe of my clawed hand, his weapon is knocked away, sent skidding across the rain-soaked pavement. My other claw finds its mark, sinking into his armored torso as if it were made of paper. In a swift, brutal motion, I hoist him off his feet and slam him onto the slick cobblestones. His life fades rapidly, his wide, terrified eyes staring blankly into the storm-laden sky.

The sudden, violent end of their comrade finally draws the attention of the remaining soldiers. Their task of eliminating the civilians momentarily forgotten, they spin towards me, their faces twisting into masks of horror. Their hands, white-knuckled and shaking, clutch their rifles as they aim at this new, monstrous threat. Rainwater trickles down the cold metal barrels of their weapons, each droplet echoing the ticking clock of their impending doom. Their hesitation, however, seals their fate. Capitalizing on their shock, I launch myself at them, cutting a swath through their ranks with terrifying speed and deadly precision.

The first soldier's life is extinguished in an instant, a swift swipe across his throat releasing a gruesome arc of crimson. Not even the chance to release a pained gasp. In the same motion, I move onto the second, my claws effortlessly piercing his armor and sinking deep into his chest. His gasping breaths quickly become ragged, then fall silent, his lifeblood ebbing away in the rain-soaked square.

While the violent spectacle unfolds, a shrill wail cuts through the air. It's the cry of an infant, a raw sound of pure innocence in stark contrast to the horror around us. I see a figure darting from the crowd, a man rushing towards the lifeless form of the mother and her still-crying child. With a swift scoop, he gathers the terrified infant into his arms and bolts away.

As the second soldier collapses and I shift my focus to the third, a familiar voice causes me to pause momentarily. "Steve?" It's Sarah. Emerging from the crowd, her eyes lock with mine. A flash of recognition crosses her features, quickly replaced by abject horror. My gut churns at the sight of her terror, a painful reminder of the monster I've become. Her breath hitches, her hands fly to her mouth. "No... it can't be," she whispers, shaking her head in disbelief.

No, Sarah, it's...' I try to speak, but my voice emerges as a harsh rasp, unrecognizable as my own.

"He's gone, Sarah, we have to go now!" the fireman's firm voice echoes through the square, recognizing the urgency of the situation, pulling Sarah away from the grisly scene and me. His urgency seems to shake Sarah from her stupor, and they disappear back into the crowd.

Returning my attention to the third soldier, I see him attempting to flee, terror etched across his face. My clawed hand snags his ankle, dragging him back into my reach. His terrified screams fill the air, but they are abruptly silenced as my claws find their mark.

The commander, the final figure still standing, fumbles in panic with his rifle, desperately struggling to reload. His eyes, wide with horror, flicker over the scene of his fallen men and he staggers back. The authority that once defined him has evaporated, replaced now by raw, unabashed terror. I surge towards him, my clawed hand honed in on his heart. His scream of terror is choked off abruptly as my claws slice through both armor and flesh. A single, violent spasm wracks his body before he crumples lifelessly to the ground, a gruesome spectacle of the brutal fallout from their ill-fated orders.

As the brutal carnage subsides, the surviving civilians seize their fleeting chance, slipping away into the shadowy labyrinth of the city's alleys. They leave me standing in isolation amid the stark aftermath, a solitary figure bathed in the harsh glow of scattered fires. An oppressive silence descends on the battlefield, punctuated only by the plaintive patter of raindrops on the debris-strewn landscape. My mind reels, wrestling with the tumult of conflicting emotions born from the devastation I've inflicted, the lives I've extinguished.

The crisp autumn wind whispers against my skin, a stark reminder of life within a shell governed by the relentless virus. As the bloodlust gradually fades, my body reverts to its zombie state, and my consciousness is once again trapped within. My form transforms back, the monstrous claws receding. The gunshot wounds inflicted upon me during the battle begin to heal, the torn flesh knitting itself back together in a disturbing display of the infection's regenerative capabilities.

I glance at the fallen civilians, relieved not to find Sarah or the fireman among them. The heaviness of my first steps speaks to the pathogen's limitations and the toll the transformation has taken on my body. Despite the horror enveloping me, I push forward, drawn by the faint scent of Sarah. Each step feels heavy, as if I'm wading through an unseen morass—a haunting indication of the parasite controlling my movements. My body, once again commandeered, leaves the square and ventures deeper into the city's heart.

The once bustling streets have transformed into a maze of devastation, littered with the grim aftermath of the pandemic's brutal touch. Burned-out vehicles pepper the roads, their metal skeletons twisted and charred. Storefronts that once displayed colorful wares now lie shattered, their interiors ransacked and strewn across the sidewalk.

Corpses, both human and undead, are scattered haphazardly about, silent witnesses to the recent carnage. Some are horrendously mutilated, others lie in pools of their own blood, their faces frozen in their last moments of terror. The scenes are gruesome, a chilling reflection of the city's rapid descent into chaos.

At the edge of my senses, I perceive the rank stench of decay. It's repulsive, an affront to the memories of fragrant gardens and fresh rain—a dreadful signature of the horror I've become. The sight of my reflection in a puddle, cast in the ethereal glow of a flickering streetlight, is a poignant punch to my gut. A monstrous creature returns my gaze, with lifeless eyes and a visage marred by death. The reality of my transformation crashes into me, threatening to drown the last vestiges of my humanity.

A scorched ArcticAde billboard stands out, a stark contrast against the surrounding ruins. A surge of memories flood in. The radio ads with their catchy slogan: Unleash the Chill Within! Officer Havilland's enthusiasm for the new soda at the police department, "This water is a game changer, guys. I've replaced all my regular sodas with it." Sarah's words echo in my head too, "I've ordered dozens of bottles, Steve. You should try it," she had told me. But I'd always preferred tap water. I never had a taste for the 'miracle' sodas.

Then it hits me. The unbitten, infected jogger clutching an ArcticAde bottle, the fridge at the first murder scene overflowing with the same brand, and every subsequent crime scene I'd visited had at least one of these bottles present. Could it be that the Arctic ice used in the drink harbored a long-dormant pathogen, now reawakened? Was ArcticAde the unsuspecting vessel of this outbreak? The implications are profound and terrifying. The very drink I dismissed could be the key to understanding, perhaps even halting, this apocalyptic nightmare.

I'm struck by a harrowing thought. If ArcticAde is the cause, Sarah will turn into a zombie too, even without a bite. The soldiers must have known this, explaining their ruthless extermination of civilians. Panic and determination surge within me. Despite being trapped in this beastly body, I must uncover the truth behind ArcticAde and save Sarah. Each heavy step reaffirms my resolve to halt this horrifying contagion.

Suddenly, a sharp, searing pain pierces my left chest, just above my heart. I want to scream in agony, but only a loud, angry growl escapes my lips. Looking down, I see an arrow lodged in me, protruding from both the front and back of my body. Blood drips onto the pavement beneath me. A voice rings out from behind, "Stay down, you monster!"

My pathogen-controlled body, now consumed with rage, scans the area for the source of the threat. I spot a man armed with a scoped hunting crossbow, desperately trying to reload it with his bare hands. He struggles to pull the string back, clearly unprepared for the reality of reloading such a weapon.

As I continue to growl in pain and anger, my body rips the arrow from my chest, causing me to silently scream as the pain intensifies. My body begins to heal, and in a display of vengeful fury, I lunge toward the man.

The survivor, now panicking, pulls out a cocking rope from his pocket, likely the tool he used to load the crossbow initially. But his lack of skill and the pressure of the situation cause him to fumble, losing precious time. As he struggles with the rope, he shouts, "Just stay away!"

Adopting a menacing, predatory stride, I reduce the gap between the survivor and myself. A shift in the air occurs—a scent that triggers an aggressive response within me. Hunger gnaws at my insides, like a beast clawing for release, demanding sustenance. Its roar drowns out reason, leading to a constant internal tug-of-war between primal need and the lingering remnants of my humanity. I assume the survivor must have a compatible blood type, perhaps AB+, as this heightens the urge to bite. Despite the efforts of my conscious mind to resist the bloodlust and halt the impending assault, the virus's control over me proves too strong, and I can only watch helplessly as the scene unfolds. The survivor shouts, "Stay back! I don't want to hurt you!"

As the virus-controlled body prepares to deliver a lethal bite to the survivor's neck, I engage in a desperate internal battle to regain control, mentally striving to halt the infection's directive, no matter the cost. The internal battle rages within me, my willpower clashing with the malevolent force that has taken over. The survivor, trembling beneath my grasp, pleads with a shaky voice, "Please, don't do this!" The attack stops abruptly, mere inches away from the survivor's vulnerable flesh. The tangible rage and hatred of the pathogen surge within me, its fury seemingly directed at my defiance of its bloodthirsty desires.

The survivor's eyes widen with fear, reflecting the terror he feels in the face of death. My sudden cessation of the assault provides a crucial window of opportunity for him. He wastes no time in shoving me away with all his might, breaking free from my grasp. As I stumble backward, disoriented by the sudden release of control, I lose my balance and crash into a metal trash bin. The impact sends a jolt of pain through my skull, and I fall into a cold, murky puddle.

Regaining his composure, the survivor yells, "Stay away from me, monster!" before bolting away at a breakneck pace, disappearing into the rain-drenched alley. His footsteps splash loudly on the wet pavement, and the steady downpour intensifies the sense of urgency as he navigates through the narrow, shadowy passageway. The frosty wind whistles through the abandoned buildings, while the distant rumble of thunder echoes ominously in the stormy night, heightening the tension and fear that permeate the atmosphere.

Though I have managed to prevent the attack, I am left drained and disoriented, swaying unsteadily on my feet. The struggle for control has taken its toll, and I wonder how much longer I can continue to resist the infection's constant drive to consume and destroy. In response to my defiance, the pathogen releases a loud, angry growl, a chilling reminder of the ever-present threat it poses.

As I struggle to maintain my control, the virus persistently pushes back, slowly regaining its grip on my body. My weakened willpower wanes, and I feel my resistance begin to crumble under the weight of the infection's incessant desire to consume. My body starts to take shaky steps forward, splashing through puddles as the rain continues to pour down.

In this tense battle of wills, I can sense the pathogen's wrath and rage directed squarely at me. It's as if it has become an entity of its own, seeking to punish me for defying its control. My pathogen-controlled body stumbles toward the brick wall of a nearby house. I'm left wondering what's happening, and then, in a swift, brutal motion, the infection commands my body to headbutt the wall with tremendous force. The pain is immense, and I can feel blood splattering across the cold, unforgiving surface.

The wound begins to heal almost immediately – a grotesque display of the infection's power and the unnatural resilience it has granted me. But the pathogen is not satisfied with a single strike. It forces my body to headbutt the wall again and again, each impact a devastating blow intended to crush my spirit and snuff out any remaining resistance.

With each collision, my vision blurs, and my grip on consciousness slips away. After the fourth excruciating hit, I finally succumb to the darkness, losing all awareness within the confines of my virus-controlled body. And yet, somewhere deep within, the last ember of my resolve still flickers, refusing to be extinguished entirely.

7

Once again, I find myself trapped in the throes of a fever dream. I'm standing in a surreal meat factory, a place where human bodies hang from hooks, encased in grimy meatbags. Sarah's desperate pleas for help reach my ears, her voice echoing and distorted, yet unmistakable. Her words bounce off the walls, adding to the disorientation of this nightmarish place.

"Steve!" she cries out, her voice trembling with fear. "Please, help me! I don't know where I am!"

The urgency in her voice propels me forward through the labyrinth of hanging meatbags, a desperate search for her amidst this morbid setting. My heart pounds, with anxiety and fear nipping at the edges of my courage.

"Sarah!" I shout back, my voice cracking with the strain. "I'm coming! Just hang on!"

Her sobs and whimpers reverberate around me, fueling my frantic search. As I follow the sound of Sarah's voice, I reach a meatbag that seems to be the source of her cries. With trembling hands, I pull it open, only for the lifeless and horrific body of the little girl from the playground to fall out. The sight is heart-wrenching, but it's not Sarah. The echoes of Sarah's pleas for help, still haunting the air, now seem to originate from another direction.

I force myself to continue, navigating the maze of meatbags, each time reaching one that I believe holds Sarah captive. But every time I open one, a familiar face from the onslaught tumbles out, disfigured and horrifying. The sight of these tragic victims fills me with guilt, a heavy burden I cannot escape. As the lead of the investigation, I feel responsible for their deaths, for their transformation into these monstrous beings. Each of them serves as a painful reminder of my failure to protect them and to save them from this nightmarish fate.

Still, Sarah's voice echoes from somewhere else, further away, and I can't give up on her. The weight of my guilt and the tireless pursuit of her salvation drive me forward, pushing me through the seemingly endless labyrinth of swaying, moaning meatbags.

"Steve, please!" Sarah's voice implores, growing weaker with each passing moment.

Determination fuels me as I push through the nightmarish landscape, desperate to save her from this hellish prison. Each new direction her voice comes from only intensifies my resolve, and I refuse to give up, no matter how many horrific bodies I uncover.

As I weave my way through the gruesome maze, an array of odors assaults my senses. The pungent scent of rotting flesh, the metallic tang of blood, and the nauseating smell of decay threaten to overwhelm me. In the midst of this olfactory chaos, I desperately try to hone in on Sarah's scent, to locate her in this nightmarish landscape.

With every step, I feel the weight of time bearing down on me, the sense of urgency growing stronger. I need to find her, to save her from this hellish place, but the path seems endless, the meatbags swaying and creaking as if taunting me in my search. Despite the suffocating dread that clings to me like a second skin, I refuse to give up. I will find her, no matter the cost.

The fragrance becomes more potent, guiding me in the right direction, giving me a renewed sense of hope. I pick up speed, running through the labyrinth of meatbags, my heart pounding with the need to find her. As I race towards the source of her scent, something eerie and unnatural begins to happen. The bodies in the meatbags start to move, their limbs twitching and jerking as if animated by some unseen force. Soon, they are running alongside me, their ghastly forms filling the air with the sound of meat and sinew slapping against each other.

I find myself sprinting through a horrifying gauntlet of hundreds of reanimated meatbags, their macabre movements propelling me forward. The terror of the scene only serves to strengthen my resolve; I have to reach Sarah before it's too late, before whatever force animates these corpses finds her too.

As the scent of Sarah grows stronger and stronger, it feels as though I'm finally closing in on her. At the same time, the growling of the running meatbags becomes louder and louder, their horrifying chorus surrounding me like a cacophony of nightmares. It's as if the very world around me is trying to deter my progress, to keep me from saving her.

Yet, just as the scent and growls reach a fever pitch, my surroundings begin to distort and warp. The horrifying figures, their grim gestures, the sheer terror of the scene, all melt away like a fevered hallucination. As one nightmare dissolves, I awaken into the chilling embrace of another.

I find myself still racing alongside the horde, our once isolated group now converging with countless others. The city lies in smoldering ruins, and we've formed a massive swarm of hundreds of zombies. Among us, many have mutated into indescribable monstrosities; some bear strange bone growths and wicked claws, while others are twisted abominations with writhing tentacles and pulsating tumors. The rain has finally ceased, leaving the air heavy with moisture and the streets littered with puddles that reflect the chaotic scene. As our swarm trudges through the soaked ruins, the sound of splashing water punctuates the air, adding a surreal ambience to our relentless march.

From somewhere ahead, the scent of Sarah beckons me, a faint yet unmistakable trace that persists despite the nightmarish surroundings. It wasn't just a dream; her presence lingers in the air, drawing me towards the direction the horde is racing. This realization fills me with dread, as I know that nothing might be able to stop this swarm from reaching her. The weight of responsibility settles upon my shoulders, and I am more determined than ever to find her and protect her from the impending danger.

As I glance at my body, I notice that it has gradually regained a semblance of normalcy. The newfound power coursing through me remains, however, fueling a burgeoning belief that my body is starting to conquer the disease, or perhaps even assimilate it. This glimmer of hope ignites my determination, and I cling to it with all my might.

From a distance, I hear the distinct roar of combat aircraft, my eyes drawn to the sight of A-10 Warthogs streaking across the sky. I recognize them from the military airshows that Sarah and I used to attend together. The A-10s, with their distinct shape and imposing presence, had always been my favorite, symbolizing power and precision. Despite their menacing appearance, they seemed to dance gracefully through the heavens, performing their demonstration flights to the powerful and triumphant notes of Vincent Frates' "March of Glory." The majestic theme, played by a full orchestra and drums with a military rhythm, resonated in the air, creating an atmosphere of awe and pride, evoking memories of those thrilling airshows we once enjoyed.

As the swarm pushes forward, we arrive at a vast opening on the outskirts of the city. We march onto a six-lane freeway that leads up to a massive bridge, connecting the urban expanse with the rural countryside beyond. It seems the swarm is intent on leaving the city through this passage, seeking to spread its terror to new territories.

The military, however, has a different agenda. Soldiers, outfitted in tactical gear and bristling with weaponry, secure their positions along the bridge, taking cover behind sandbag fortifications and makeshift barricades. Main battle tanks stand in intimidating support, their turrets rotating ominously. Other armored vehicles form a formidable defensive barrier. The faces of the soldiers display an uneasy blend of determination and apprehension, reflecting their deep understanding of the situation's severity and the critical importance of their mission to hold the line.

Serving as the final battleground, the bridge presents a decisive confrontation between humanity and the mass of the risen horde. With abandoned vehicles and civilian corpses strewn about, the scene grimly illustrates the soldiers' attempts to prevent the panicked crowd from breaching their defensive line. Unaware civilians continue to sprint toward the barricades, facing threats from both the undead and a military intent on preventing the contagion's spread beyond the city. Amidst the ceaseless advance of the swarm, fueled by a primal need to feed and multiply, I find myself torn between two worlds, fervently seeking a way to rescue the one I love and end the all-consuming nightmare.

The A-10s circle overhead, their engines thundering like a harbinger of doom. I recall the adrenaline rush that accompanied the aircraft's breathtaking maneuvers during airshows. Sarah would grip my hand in excitement as we marveled at the spectacle, our chests reverberating with each rapid flyby. The exhilaration and unity of those airshows, now a distant memory, serve as a stark counterpoint to the havoc and disorder that the A-10s inflict upon the city below.

The Warthogs unleash a barrage of Hydra missiles, perhaps indicating that the military wants to avoid excessive collateral damage. As the missiles pass high over my head and explode way behind me, seemingly attempting to chop the horde into smaller waves with gaps in between. Plumes of smoke and debris rise from the battered cityscape, obscuring the sun and casting an eerie pall over the ruined metropolis.

As the aircraft circle back, they descend lower and lower, their intent clear. The Gatling guns beneath their fuselages begin to spin, the metal barrels glinting in the scarce sunlight that manages to break through the haze. In a matter of seconds, a torrential hailstorm of bullets is unleashed upon the relentless tide of zombies below.

Bullets whiz past me, some narrowly missing my flesh. I can feel the searing heat of their trajectories. The overwhelming noise of gunfire and explosions is deafening, drowning out the groans and snarls of the infected. Around me, countless zombies crumble, their reanimated forms dismembered by the relentless fire, limbs severed, decaying bodies sent sprawling to the ground. The battlefield air is thick with the acrid scent of gunpowder and scorched flesh, a nauseating perfume that lingers heavily. Amidst the chaos, I find myself mesmerized by the deadly ballet of the A-10s as they swoop and strike in their lethal dance, attempting to quell the onslaught of the walkers.

Despite the overwhelming firepower brought to bear against them, the zombie mass continues to press forward, their single-minded relentlessness to feed driving them ever onward. The A-10s' ferocious assault, however, has at least slowed the advance, buying precious time for the beleaguered defenders on the bridge.

I struggle internally, torn between the instinctual drive to protect Sarah and the rational knowledge that I must find safety. My mind screams for my body to obey, but my limbs seem to have a mind of their own, inexorably drawn to the scent of Sarah that hangs in the air, tantalizing and tormenting me. No matter how hard I try to resist, my body refuses to heed my desperate pleas, driven by an inexplicable urge to find her, regardless of the danger that awaits.

My heart pounds in my chest, a persistent drumbeat of fear and anxiety, as I grapple with my own lack of control. The storm of emotions raging within me only serves to fuel my determination to regain command over my body and find a way to escape this nightmarish reality.

As I stumble forward, driven by forces beyond my understanding, I cannot help but wonder what lies at the heart of this irresistible pull towards Sarah. Is it my love for her, somehow amplified by the virus coursing through my veins, or is it something far more sinister, born of the darkness that now holds me in its thrall? The answer, like so much else in this shattered world, remains elusive, leaving me to cling to the hope that I may yet find a way to resist the siren call of the horde and reclaim the life that was stolen from me.

As the battle rages on, I suddenly become aware of a deep, rumbling sound in the distance. Through the chaos, I spot some M1A2 Abrams tanks rolling into view, their massive treads churning up debris as they advance. I remember how they had always captivated my attention at the military shows, their imposing armored bodies a symbol of raw power and force. Sarah and I would marvel at their size and strength, awed by the destructive potential they possessed.

The tanks take their positions, barrels aimed and turrets traversing, ready to unleash their devastating firepower on the advancing horde. Suddenly, they freeze in place. The horde inches closer, but the tanks remain still. Then, without warning, they fire.

Their cannons hurl explosive payloads that echo through the scarred cityscape, while the mounted machine guns add a rapid staccato to the symphony of destruction. Their bullets tear through the undead with ruthless efficiency. Each successive blast sends tremors through the ground, as high-explosive shells slice through the air and decimate clusters of zombies. Many around me fall in the crossfire, their reanimated forms shredded by the tank's mighty ordnance. The air fills with the acrid scent of burning flesh and the chilling sound of shattering bone, weaving an unnerving tapestry of death and devastation.

Miraculously, I manage to evade the hail of deadly projectiles, my body instinctively darting through the chaos. The scent of Sarah, ever-present in my mind, continues to guide me, propelling me forward even as the world crumbles around me.

As the conflict intensifies, the distinctive roar of the A-10 Warthogs' engines fills the air, signaling their return for another attack run. Though I cannot see them through the smoke-choked sky, their presence is unmistakable. The remaining zombies, including the grotesque mutated monstrosities, persist in their unyielding pursuit of the living, seemingly unfazed by the military's ferocious assault.

Suddenly, I hear the unmistakable sound of the A-10s' Gatling guns – a guttural, rapid brrrrrrrrrrrr that sends chills down my spine. In an instant, a hailstorm of bullets sweeps through the swarm of walkers, passing perilously close to me. The incessant onslaught of gunfire tears through the zombies around me, leaving a trail of shattered and lifeless corpses in its wake.

One of the A-10s swoops in low, its Gatling gun unleashing a lethal rain of bullets upon the throng of the ghouls. In response, an unusual zombie lumbers forward from the pack. Disturbingly bloated, two large, pulsating tumors filled with an ominous liquid protrude from its body. The creature retches and, with sickening precision, launches a stream of this liquid towards the aircraft.

Upon impact, the substance immediately begins to eat through the A-10's right wing and engine, dissolving the metal at an astonishing rate. It becomes clear that the creature's tumors contain a potent acid, concentrated enough to corrode even the Warthog's armored exterior. As the acid takes its toll, the engine ignites, causing a catastrophic failure that sends a fireball coursing along the wing before it tears away from the aircraft entirely. Emitting a tortured screech of rending metal and trailing a plume of black smoke, the crippled aircraft begins its uncontrollable descent, spiraling toward the imposing structure of the bridge.

In a desperate, last-ditch effort, the pilot tries to eject from the doomed aircraft, but there isn't enough altitude for the ejection seat to clear the wreckage. Tragically, the pilot's body smashes into the bridge's pavement, leaving no hope for survival. As the aircraft collides with the tall towers of the bridge, a fiery explosion erupts, engulfing the main and supporting cables in a blaze of destruction. Despite the devastating impact, the bridge remains intact, albeit heavily damaged and weakened.

The deafening explosion from the downed A-10 casts a sinister glow over the battlefield. The wreckage from the explosion falls onto the bridge, burying some soldiers beneath the twisted metal and debris. This catastrophic scene serves as a haunting testament to the immense power and danger this undead onslaught represents, and the sacrifices made in the struggle against this nightmarish threat. But the realization that even the military's most fearsome weapons are not immune to the wrath of these abominations only serves to amplify the hopelessness that pervades the air.

In the midst of the chaos, a sniper positioned behind the barricade spots the acid-spitter zombie that brought down the A-10.

Taking careful aim, the sharpshooter fires a single, precise shot that pierces the creature's skull. As the zombie falls backward, the potent acid begins to accumulate within its body. Moments later, the bloated corpse explodes, showering nearby zombies with the deadly substance. The acid rapidly melts through their flesh, even dissolving their bones, reducing the once-menacing creatures to unrecognizable puddles of goo.

As the remaining A-10s assess the grave threat posed by the mutated monstrosities, they make the tactical decision to retreat. The formidable aircrafts turn and ascend rapidly, their powerful engines roaring as they disappear into the smoke-choked skies above, leaving the soldiers on the ground to face the relentless horde.

Amid the chaos, I finally catch sight of Sarah, her figure cutting through the haze of destruction like a beacon of hope. She is still accompanied by the valiant fireman, both of them desperately trying to find a path to safety. However, they find themselves cornered – on one side, the military forces who, as they have already experienced, seem intent on eliminating civilians alongside the undead threat; on the other, the inexorable swarm of zombies advancing unyieldingly.

As I draw closer, I can see the desperation etched on both Sarah's and the fireman's faces as they come to the grim realization that there may be no way out of this nightmarish scenario. Their eyes dart frantically, searching for any possible escape route, but finding none. The situation deteriorates further as the military starts firing on civilians too, considering them expendable in their frantic efforts to contain the undead swarm. A majority of the civilians fall to the initial barrage of gunfire, their hopelessness hanging heavily in the air. The stark reality of their precarious situation only fuels my determination to reach Sarah, even as I grapple with the turmoil raging within me.

Through the haze of smoke and chaos, I see the fireman grab Sarah's arm and pull her towards the cover of a burnt-out truck. They huddle together, Sarah covering her ears and crying hysterically as the mass of ghouls approaches from one side and bullets whiz past them from the other. It's painfully clear that neither of them wants to die, but with every passing moment, their chances for survival seem to dwindle.

Despite the barrage of gunfire and the continuous advance of the walking corpses, something within me refuses to give up. My body responds to this fierce determination, and I find myself running faster than ever, every fiber of my being straining to reach Sarah and the fireman before it's too late. As I draw nearer, I can feel the raw power coursing through my veins, propelling me forward with a speed and strength I never knew I possessed. The carnage around me fades into a blur as I focus solely on reaching them, driven by an unyielding desire to protect the ones I love.

The Abrams tanks persist in their unyielding attack, their formidable cannons thundering as they fire round after round of high-explosive shells into the unstoppable flood of walkers. The tanks' overwhelming firepower seems to be the only thing keeping the monstrous wave from reaching Sarah and the fireman. Yet, despite the tanks' devastating assault, the initial wave of mutated monstrosities manages to close the gap, their grotesque shapes casting a sinister shadow against the chaos that surrounds them.

These horrifying creatures, seemingly immune to the force of the tank shells, charge towards the armored vehicles with astonishing speed and ferocity.

As I watch the scene unfold, I notice something peculiar – the mutated zombies seem to bypass Sarah and the fireman, leaping over their makeshift shelter as they continue their advance. In the midst of the chaos, this strikes me as strange, as if the priorities of these monstrosities have shifted. It's as though their focus has moved from the pursuit of human prey to confronting the military forces that stand in their way.

This unexpected turn of events provides a small window of opportunity for Sarah and the fireman. The persistent onslaught of the swarm momentarily held at bay, they now have a chance to seek safety, if only they can find a way through the chaos that surrounds them. As my body continues to race towards them, driven by an inexplicable compulsion, I can't help but wonder if I will be able to protect them or if I'll succumb to the hunger that still lingers within me.

With brutal efficiency, the monstrosities begin to dismantle the tanks. Their bone-crushing claws tear through the armored plating like paper, while their tentacles wrap around the turrets, wrenching them free with horrifying ease. The once-invincible Abrams tanks are reduced to smoldering wreckage in a matter of minutes, their crews meeting a gruesome fate at the hands of these hideous abominations.

Just as it seems that all hope is lost, a second line of main battle tanks, accompanied by other fighting vehicles rolls into view from behind the initial line of defense. They swiftly take up positions and unleash a barrage of powerful shells, their cannons roaring in unison. The ground trembles beneath their assault, shaking the very foundations of the ravaged city.

Simultaneously, AH-64D Apache helicopters rise from both sides of the bridge, a favorite of mine that Sarah never quite shared my enthusiasm for, bringing to mind a particular memory. I recall a time when Sarah and I were relaxing in my apartment after a long day of work. I had just finished putting together a small model of an Apache helicopter, and proudly displayed it on the shelf.

"What's that?" Sarah asked, pointing at the model with a raised eyebrow.

"That's an Apache helicopter. Isn't it cool?" I replied, my enthusiasm for the aircraft shining through.

Sarah pursed her lips and tilted her head, examining the model with a critical eye. "Ugly combat bug," she said with a hint of disapproval. I laughed at her description, but I could tell she wasn't as fascinated by it as I was.

Now, as the real Apaches rise from both sides of the bridge, their powerful rotors slicing through the smog-filled air, I can't help but think of Sarah's disdain for the aircraft. Despite her lack of enthusiasm for the "ugly combat bug," its presence is a welcome sight for the survivors in the midst of battle.

As they ascend, they immediately open fire with their 30mm chain guns, weaving through the chaos with deadly precision as they rain down destruction upon the undead swarm. The helicopter pilots expertly maneuver their machines, their skill evident in the graceful arcs and swoops they execute amidst the unfolding pandemonium, providing a glimmer of hope amidst the carnage. One of the Apaches hovers right above Sarah and the fireman, casting an imposing shadow over their precarious shelter, like a guardian angel in this hellish landscape.

Suddenly, a spine-spitter zombie takes aim at the Apache, launching a barrage of spines towards the helicopter. Despite its efforts, the spines merely bounce off the Apache's thick armor, causing no damage. In response, the Apache unleashes a barrage of unguided Hydra rockets at the spine-spitter and the sea of undead beyond. Some of these rockets narrowly pass over my head, their terrifying whistle announcing their deadly presence, like a chorus of vengeful spirits.

The missiles explode behind me, sending a shockwave through the air and a deafening roar that rattles my bones. The devastation they cause within the mass of walkers is immense, as countless zombies are ripped to pieces by the sheer force of the blasts. Flung about in every direction, decaying limbs and flesh contribute to a chilling spectacle of devastation, heightened by the unyielding assault of the Apache helicopters. The explosions ignite the morning sky, casting ghastly silhouettes across the war-torn landscape, creating an eerily beautiful yet horrifying panorama.

However, the horde refuses to go down without a fight. A particularly daring Apache helicopter strays too close to the frontlines in its pursuit of the undead, and in a horrifying display of agility and strength, one of the tentacled monstrosities shoots its sharp tentacles upwards, acting like harpoons as they pierce through the aircraft's armor. The sound of shattering metal fills the air as the Apache's hull is punctured, and the tentacle zombie uses its monstrous appendages to yank the helicopter out of the sky.

As the helicopter plummets to the ground, its flaming wreckage crashes into the battlefield below. As it hits the ground and turns on its side, the rotor slices through several zombies before the Apache erupts into a fiery explosion. In response to the sudden attack, the other Apache that was hovering above Sarah and the fireman quickly strafes away, maintaining a cautious distance from the walker onslaught to avoid suffering a similar fate.

Seeing the chaos momentarily shift the focus of both the military and the zombies, I recognize a fleeting window of opportunity to reach Sarah. My body races with incredible speed, propelling me through the destruction and death that surrounds us. As I weave through the hordes of undead and dodge the deadly crossfire, I feel an indomitable resolve surging within me, fueled by my unwavering determination to protect Sarah at all costs.

As I draw closer to her, my heart swells with an overwhelming mixture of hope and fear. The world around us seems to blur and fade, leaving only the two of us standing in the eye of this apocalyptic storm. My legs pump furiously, each stride bringing me closer to the woman I love, the woman I would do anything to save from the horrors that now threaten to consume her.

Meanwhile, one of the grotesque tumor monsters begins to swell and pulsate, as if it's about to burst. It charges towards the line of tanks with reckless abandon, seemingly impervious to the continuous barrage of gunfire. As it reaches the tanks, the monster explodes in a gruesome spectacle of blood and viscera. The shockwave from the detonation is powerful enough to shatter the formation, throwing the tanks into disarray and momentarily breaking the line.

The battle between the zombie swarm and the military forces rages on, a chaotic dance of death and destruction. The conflict is brutal and unforgiving, and though the tide seems to be turning, it's evident that neither side will emerge from this fight unscathed.

Slowly but surely, the combined firepower of the tanks, helicopters, and foot soldiers begins to turn the tide. The monstrosities, once thought invincible, succumb to the unending hail of shells, missiles, and gunfire. The foot soldiers fire continuously at everything that moves beyond the barricade, both the remaining civilians and zombies alike, desperate to contain the threat. Their monstrous forms shatter and burn, the once-terrifying creatures reduced to smoldering heaps of gore and twisted flesh.

As the military forces continue to gain ground against the walkers, the A-10 Warthogs make a sudden, unexpected return. The aircraft burst through the heavy clouds, their silhouettes stark against the turbulent sky. They swoop down for one last, devastating pass, their Gatling guns spitting out a lethal stream of bullets that tear through the ranks of the remaining ghouls. The shots miss me, but I fear that my luck will run out before I reach Sarah.

I leap into action, using the roofs of abandoned cars as stepping stones to rapidly close the distance between us. Each powerful jump propels me closer to Sarah, and the battle around us reaches a fever pitch. Sarah lets out a terrified scream at my sudden appearance, her eyes wide with fear.

Determined to protect Sarah, the fireman positions himself between her and me, raising his fire axe in a defensive stance. "Stay back!" he bellows at me, his voice echoing in the abandoned street. "I won't let you harm her!" Each word punctuates his determination, highlighting the fact that he's willing to risk everything for Sarah's safety. Despite the fear in his eyes, his resolute courage shines through, a clear reflection of his unwavering commitment to his duty.

As the axe descends, I feel a remarkable shift within me – my body and consciousness finally in sync once more. In a display of regained control, I react with lightning-fast reflexes, seizing the fireman's wrist mid-swing and twisting it sharply. The fire axe clatters to the ground, and with a swift motion, I grab the fireman's neck and knock him unconscious. I refrain from taking his life, fully aware that he is a protector, not an enemy.

The Warthogs' engines roar overhead, bullets whistling past amidst the tumultuous battle. The firepower decimates the zombie horde, scattering their once formidable mass.

I try to speak to Sarah, to reassure her that it's me, but my words manifest as an inhuman snarl, underscoring my monstrous metamorphosis. Seeing this, Sarah's fear seems to overwhelm her, and she gives up, collapsing to her knees in despair. I move closer to her, my heart aching with the need to protect her.

The distinctive sound of the A-10s fills the air one last time, but the gunfire has ceased – their ammunition reserves are exhausted. The roar of their engines reverberates through the city, signaling the conclusion of their mission. As they climb against the backdrop of the morning sky, one Warthog performs a perfect victory roll, its silhouette briefly shadowing the break of day in a triumphant salute to their hard-won success.

Securing Sarah in my hold, I sense her body shivering against mine, succumbing to the tidal wave of fear and sorrow. A distinctive scent, hitherto unnoticed, now fills my senses - the unmistakable marker of infection. She's already in the grip of the virus, her remaining time slipping away. An inner voice offers a wild remedy: to bite her, sharing the peculiar force within me that has, thus far, kept my own transformation in check. Caught in the storm of conflicting emotions, I ready myself to confront an unthinkable decision.

The fear and confusion in Sarah's eyes are heart-wrenching, and my need to protect her is overwhelming. Filled with a compulsion to bite her, hoping that the pathogen failing to control me might save her too, I brace myself and sink my teeth into her forearm. Sarah screams in pain, resisting the bite. Tears stream down her terrified face as she pleads, "No, please, don't do this!"

The taste of iron floods my mouth, the unmistakable tang of blood. My tongue recoils from the bitter aftertaste. Yet a perverse part of me hungers for more, a remnant of the disease's insidious design. Eventually, I release her, hoping my actions might spare her in the end.

Sarah's eyes flutter shut as she collapses into my hold, the torment and terror overwhelming her. As I cradle her, I perceive a subtle quivering course through her body, a subcutaneous ripple signifying an inward shift. Perhaps a transformation prompted by my bite is underway. A desperate hope dawns within me, praying that this change will be her salvation, not a sentence to an existence more monstrous than death.

The chaotic ballet of battle continues to unfurl around us, but my world narrows down to Sarah alone. Each passing second, agonizingly slow, amplifies the suspense - a torturous wait to discern her fate. But as time ticks on, there's no grotesque mutation, no monstrous outburst. She remains, achingly, human.

In that moment, something shifts in the behavior of the remaining zombies. I sense it—an eerie, unnatural change. The remnant of the horde turns its attention to us, attacking us directly instead of focusing on the military forces that continue firing at them. I don't understand this sudden shift in their behavior, but my instincts take over.

My body endures another swift mutation as my razor-sharp claws extend, readying myself to defend Sarah against the living dead onslaught. However, this time, something feels distinctly different. Previously, while the virus seemed to puppeteer my actions, I managed to exercise some control over my mutated form. Now, it feels as if, for the first time, I am truly acting on my own volition, resolved to protect Sarah, no matter the cost.

As the zombies close in, I unleash my newfound power, tearing through their ranks with ferocious speed and strength. The battlefield becomes a blur of movement, the clash of claws and the sickening crunch of bone filling the air. But with every swing of my claws, I can't shake the feeling that something is terribly wrong, and that the consequences of my actions may be beyond my comprehension.

Another round of Apache helicopters swoop in to replace the ones that exhausted their ammo, their guns blazing as they join the fight against the swarm. Interestingly, the newly arrived Apaches seem to focus their attention on the group of zombies attacking Sarah and me, providing much-needed support as we struggle to fend off the relentless assault. Another wave of tanks and armored carriers roll in, accompanied by a flood of soldiers on foot, all working together to combat the unyielding tide of undead.

As I fight the ravenous animated corpses, the chaos of the battlefield surrounds me. The roar of the tank engines, the staccato bursts of gunfire, and the screams of the dying blend into a maelstrom of sound and fury. My primary focus, however, remains steadfastly on protecting Sarah and the unconscious fireman.

From the corner of my eye, I notice one of the tanks swiveling its massive barrel towards me. Instinctively, I break away from the grisly melee with the zombies just as the tank opens fire, my arm morphing into a large, bony shield to place between the tank, Sarah, and the fireman.

The 120mm shell slams into the bone shield, the impact sending me flying through the air in a cloud of debris and dust. I crash to the ground, dazed and disoriented, my body aching from the tremendous force of the explosion. The sound of battle continues around me, but it gradually begins to fade, as if the military has emerged victorious. As I teeter on the edge of unconsciousness, a female voice cuts through the chaos of battle, commanding, "Stand down!" The force of the explosion has left me disoriented and lying on the bridge's asphalt, struggling to maintain my awareness.

Footsteps approach me, and the same woman speaks again, her tone intrigued: "You seem interesting." She then gives another command: "Take these three to the laboratory."

My eyes desperately try to locate Sarah amidst the chaos. My vision blurs, but I manage to catch a glimpse of her lying on the ground. My consciousness, previously dormant, fights to regain control of my mutated body. Surprisingly, my arm, which has been unresponsive and uncontrollable for the entire ordeal, now obeys my command. My trembling hand stretches out towards Sarah, my pointer finger reaching for her distant body as if trying to bridge the gap between us. Then, darkness envelops me, and I lose consciousness.

In the depths of another fever dream, I find myself standing in a barren, desolate landscape. The sky overhead is an angry, swirling maelstrom of clouds, casting a sickly, unnatural light on the scene below. Before me stands Sarah, her once beautiful face now horrific and distorted. One head, with two faces seamlessly merged together, each with its own set of eyes and mouth. The faces express different emotions, a horrifying duality that chills me to the core.

One face is twisted with pain and anguish, tear-streaked and pleading. "Why did you bite me, Steve?" it sobs, the question echoing through the eerie silence. "Why did you condemn me to this nightmare?"

The other face, however, is eerily calm and content. It smiles serenely, a twisted expression of gratitude. "Thank you, Steve," it whispers, its voice chillingly sweet. "You saved me. I couldn't have survived without you."

The two faces continue to speak, their voices overlapping and intertwining, creating a dissonant harmony that claws at my sanity. I stand frozen, unable to move or speak, as the faces of the woman I love confront me with the duality of my actions.

Sarah steps closer to me, her duality even more apparent as the distance between us diminishes. The crying, pained face seems to be reaching out to me, seeking comfort and understanding, while the other face remains joyful, a twisted grin that sends shivers down my spine. As I look into her eyes, I can't help but notice an unsettling darkness lurking behind the joy, an evil presence that fills me with a sense of foreboding.

As she moves nearer, I find myself unable to step back, my feet rooted to the ground as if by some unseen force. The dissonant voices grow louder, more insistent, and the weight of my guilt and responsibility bears down on me with increasing intensity.

"Steve, how could you?" the anguished face asks, the pain in her voice nearly unbearable to hear. "Why did you doom me to this existence?"

"Steve, you've done well," the other face chimes in, her voice sickeningly sweet and malicious. "You've ensured my survival, and for that, I am grateful."

The conflicting emotions tear at me from within, leaving me feeling lost and overwhelmed. How could I have let this happen? What have I done to the woman I love? The torment of my actions threatens to consume me, leaving me to question if I can ever find redemption or if I am forever condemned to carry the weight of my sins.

As I watch, Sarah's form begins to twist and contort, her once beautiful features distorting into something sinister and inhuman. Her eyes darken, becoming bottomless pools of malevolence, and her limbs elongate, taking on a grotesque appearance. The transformation is swift and horrifying, leaving me breathless with terror.

The terrified face screams in agony as the transformation unfolds, her desperate cries for help echoing through the nightmarish landscape. It's as if she's being devoured from within, her humanity being stripped away by the other face. The sinister visage, once hidden beneath the surface, now slowly takes over, gradually dominating her entire being.

The monstrous creature that was once Sarah now towers over me. Before I can utter a word, it reaches out and grabs my neck, its icy voice echoing as she hisses, "Now it's your turn to die." The malicious words reverberate through the oppressive atmosphere, promising a fate that I cannot comprehend but fills me with a sense of impending doom.

My eyes snap open, the unsettling nightmare fading as I find myself in an unfamiliar environment. I'm strapped to a cold, sturdy metal table within a sterile military lab, a stark contrast to the devastated cityscape I'd been navigating as a zombie. The restraints holding me are made from industrial-grade Kevlar, interwoven with metal for added durability. A line runs from a nearby medical stand into my arm, steadily pumping sedatives into my system. Despite my newfound strength, I can't break free. A deep snarl reverberates from my throat, a primal sound that permeates the cold, sterile room.

A disquieting quietude pervades my mind, akin to the calm before a storm—an unsettling silence foregrounding the war between my past self and the monster I've become. I can sense my heartbeat, a slow, irregular rhythm echoing within my chest. Each pulsation serves as a reminder of my existence on the edge, teetering between life and death.

From the corner of my eyes, I can see a soldier guarding the entrance to my room, which is poorly lit but appears to be a larger medical space capable of accommodating more than one patient. The room fills with the soft hum of medical equipment, a symphony of artificial life humming along to the beat of science. The air, cool and sterile, wraps around me like a sanitized shroud, standing in stark contrast to the chaos I had been immersed in not long ago. The presence of the guard and the clinical environment only add to the unease and tension that envelop me, making it even more difficult to understand what is happening and what my captors' intentions might be. Fear and confusion wash over me as I begin to question my newfound imprisonment. Who could have possibly captured me, and for what purpose?

A military doctor, clad in a white lab coat, steps into my line of vision, her expression a mixture of curiosity and concern. She leans over me, using a small lamp to scan my eyes with a clinical interest. "Fascinating," she murmurs, her voice a mixture of wonder and professionalism. "There's still a glimmer of consciousness in you, despite the virus." My heart leaps at her words, a small flicker of hope igniting within me. Could she possibly help me regain control of my body and rid me of the virus?

The doctor straightens up and offers a brief smile, attempting to put me at ease. "My name is Dr. Elizabeth Jennings," she introduces herself. As she leans closer, I notice the keycard hanging around her neck, confirming her name and revealing her rank as a Major in the army. "I can see you're frightened, and I want you to know that I'm here to help you, not harm you," she says. As I listen to her speak, I suddenly recognize her voice. She was the one who spared me on the battlefield, opting to capture me instead of ending my life. The realization fills me with a mixture of gratitude and unease. "If you can understand what I'm saying, please blink twice."

I focus all my energy and willpower on my eyelids, desperate to show her that I am still aware and capable of comprehending her words. With immense effort, I manage to blink twice, my heart pounding in my chest.

A smile tugs at the corner of Dr. Jennings' mouth, and she nods. "Good. I'm glad we can communicate. This is a breakthrough in our research. Most infected individuals we've encountered so far have been completely lost to the infection. But you're different. Somehow, your consciousness has managed to hold on. We don't know why, but we're determined to find out."

She pauses momentarily, appearing contemplative. "Based on our findings, the contagion either takes control of the host within two-three days or, if it fails to replicate, perishes inside the host during the same period. The compulsion to bite serves as a means for the pathogen to reproduce and ensure its survival, while eating is an innate process that sustains the host. The more bites an infected individual inflicts, the more the contagion establishes itself in the body, making the takeover process irreversible after one or two bites. However, we have yet to ascertain what factors contribute to this peculiar selection process, which determines who becomes a zombie and who ends up as prey."

Dr. Jennings furrows her brow. "According to my theory, the virus will eventually vanish within you. In your body, the parasite is basically starving to death, which is the reason for its vanishing.

But what puzzles me is how it's still dying in your body even after you bit that woman. It's like your bite didn't cause a feedback and, since you didn't eat either, your body's starvation has also weakened the infection. There must be something unique about your condition that we have yet to discover."

As I listen intently to Dr. Jennings, I can't help but wonder why my bite had no effect on Sarah. Ever since I bit her, something has felt off, and now the doctor's explanation confirms my suspicions. Desperate to share the information I've learned about the contagion, I try to form words, to speak and tell her what I know. But only savage snarls escape my mouth, the virus still maintaining a firm grasp on my body. Dr. Jennings looks at me with understanding and sympathy, realizing my struggle to communicate.

"I know you want to speak, Steve, but it's still not possible right now," she says gently. "The virus has a firm hold on you, so it may take some time for you to regain your ability to speak. Just know that you're not alone in this fight."

I wonder how she knows my name, but then Dr. Jennings pulls out my detective ID, heavily burnt around the edges and with my family name scorched unreadable, from her pocket and shows it to me. "I found this in your pocket," she explains. "It's how I know your name, Detective."

Her words fill me with a mixture of hope and trepidation. While I'm encouraged by the fact that she recognizes my consciousness and seems determined to help me, I can't help but worry about the unknown trials and experiments that may lie ahead. Regardless, one thing is clear: Dr. Jennings and her team might be my only chance to regain control of my body and put an end to this living nightmare.

Dr. Jennings continues, "Let's try to establish a simple communication method. If something I say is correct, blink once slowly. If it's false, blink twice quickly. Do you understand?"

I concentrate and blink once slowly, confirming that I understand her instructions.

"Alright, let's begin," she says, her expression focused. "Do you know the woman you were protecting?"

I think of Sarah, and the memories flood my mind – her laughter, her kindness, her love for classical music. I blink once, slowly, confirming that I know her.

"Do you know the fireman?" This time, I blink twice quickly.

Dr. Jennings seems thoughtful for a moment before asking, "Even though you don't know the fireman, you still didn't want to harm him, did you?" I blink once slowly, confirming that despite my lack of personal connection to the fireman, I didn't want to cause him harm.

Dr. Jennings finds my responses intriguing. "It's fascinating that even in this state, you're capable of love and protecting others. That's something we haven't observed before in infected individuals," she muses. Then, with a thoughtful look, she adds, "Not that we've seen such behavior from healthy individuals amidst this crisis either."

She takes a deep breath and continues, "I have some news about Sarah and Mr. Washington. They're both alive and in separate medical rooms under surveillance. The bad news is that Sarah is infected. However, for some reason, her symptoms are stable.

We believe your bite might be the reason..." Dr. Jennings hesitates and she quickly adds, "but..." She doesn't finish the thought and changes the subject. "As for Mr. Washington, he is uninfected, although he has some injuries. Thanks to your efforts to protect them, both of them are alive and in our care."

As a seasoned detective, I can sense that Dr. Jennings is not telling me everything. Her sudden change of topic and the unfinished sentence make me suspicious.

Dr. Jennings turns her attention to a clipboard, scribbling down a few observations in her neat handwriting. She flips through several pages filled with notes and diagrams, pausing occasionally to study the information before her. Eventually, she looks up from the clipboard, meeting my eyes with a cautiously optimistic expression. "While we still have much to learn and understand about this contagion, this development in your case gives us hope. We'll continue to monitor your condition closely and work to uncover the reasons behind the pathogen's retreat."

As Dr. Jennings continues to write notes, diligently recording her observations, she hums a familiar tune under her breath - a song I must have heard on the radio before. The sound is strangely comforting, reminding me of simpler times before this nightmare began.

I gradually become more aware of my body. The numbness that had engulfed my hand earlier starts to recede, replaced by a faint, tingling sensation that spreads throughout my extremities. My consciousness, previously consumed by the infection's grip, begins to recognize that my body is indeed prevailing in the battle against the disease. Hope swells within me, like a flood breaking through its barriers, as I feel the control over my body gradually returning, one small triumph at a time.

Held captive by the straps fastening me to the table, I concentrate on coordinating my fingers with the melodic rhythm of Dr. Jennings's hum. I coax them into motion, a silent plea for them to exhibit the returning control. This tingling sensation gradually radiates from my fingers, coursing into my hand, then my arm, all while my conscious will battles the insidious force that's kept me shackled for an agonizing stretch of time.

Dr. Jennings, absorbed in her notes, suddenly catches sight of my fingers moving in sync with her humming. Her eyes widen in surprise, and she quickly shifts her full attention to me. "Were you deliberately moving your hand in response to my humming? If so, please blink once to confirm."

Gathering all my strength and willpower, I blink once, confirming to her that the movement was intentional. The look of astonishment on Dr. Jennings' face is unmistakable. She pauses for a moment to process this development before speaking, "By God, I was right. It appears the infection is indeed starving and gradually retreating from your body, Steve. I firmly believe that you'll soon regain full control over your body.

Dr. Jennings glances at her watch and then back at me. "You should rest for now. I'll come back to check on you in a little while." She gives me a reassuring smile before leaving the room, the door closing behind her.

As I lie there, I try to rest, maybe even fall asleep. I can feel the numbness throughout my body slowly starting to dissipate. I focus on my arm, willing it to move as I had done with my hand earlier.

Bit by bit, I regain control over my arm, and the sensation of hope continues to grow within me. I know that I'm winning the battle against the disease, and with each passing moment, I'm getting closer to being free.

When I do fall asleep, my dreams are a blur. This time, I can't find Sarah in them, and when I awaken, I can't remember any details at all. The absence of Sarah in my dreams leaves me feeling somewhat empty, but I remind myself that she is alive and being cared for.

A few hours later, Dr. Jennings returns to the room, her eyes immediately drawn to my arm. "Steve, can you try moving your arm for me?" she asks, her voice filled with anticipation and curiosity. My first instinct is to respond verbally, but a low growl escapes my throat instead. Frustrated, I decide to simply blink once, indicating that I'm willing to give it a try.

Reading my affirmation, Dr. Jennings turns towards the soldier, her voice clear and authoritative. "Sergeant, please unstrap our friend here."

The soldier, broad-shouldered and stern-faced, immediately complies. He moves towards me, his boots making a soft, rhythmic sound against the polished tile floor. His gloved hands are surprisingly gentle as he unstraps my arm, the one that had regained movement earlier. Once my hand is free, the soldier steps back, reassuming his position by the entrance.

I concentrate and, with a renewed sense of determination, slowly lift my arm off the table, showing her the progress I've made. Dr. Jennings walks over to a nearby counter and retrieves a sheet of paper and a pen. She carefully slips the paper under my hand and elevates it so I can see what I'm writing. She places the pen in my fingers. "Let's try to communicate this way," she suggests, her eyes filled with curiosity and determination. "Write whatever you need to share with us."

Before attempting to write, I take a moment to gather all my thoughts about the case, to ensure that I convey the most crucial information. With great effort, I focus on moving my hand to write on the paper. The pen feels heavy and unwieldy in my fingers, the muscles in my hand trembling as I regain control. But, with a surge of willpower, I manage to scrawl a legible message: Bloodtypes = zomb/food, AB+ = block/cure, ArcticAde = virus.

Dr. Jennings examines the paper, her eyes widening in surprise. "Are you sure about this?" she asks, her voice filled with a mix of disbelief and intrigue.

I concentrate once again, forcing my hand to move and write my response: I'm a detective, followed by a small smiley face at the end.

Dr. Jennings looks at the message again, her eyes widening with realization. "I believe you. If this is true, it means we might be able to synthesize a cure. There's real hope now." She pauses for a moment, her expression turning serious. "You know, I've never understood why ArcticAde, a simple arctic ice soda, gained so much attention and hype in the media, even in local news. It's odd that it was limited to our city only, unavailable anywhere else or even online. If the outbreak was intentional, it would explain the peculiar marketing strategy and the sudden rise in popularity."

Her voice trails off, and it's clear that she's lost in thought, piecing together the implications of this revelation. As she does so, my mind races too, processing the sinister possibilities of a world where a seemingly harmless soda could be the catalyst for such devastation. The thought is unnerving, but at least now we have a lead – a potential way to fight back and reclaim our lives.

I gather my strength and write one more word on the paper: "Sarah?" Dr. Jennings glances at the word and hesitates for a moment before responding. "We'll talk about her later," she says, her tone cautious. This evasive answer makes me suspicious, and I can't shake the feeling that she's hiding something about Sarah's condition. Despite my concerns, I know I must focus on the information at hand and trust that Dr. Jennings will address the issue when the time is right.

As Dr. Jennings walks away, she moves towards the room's phone and dials a number. After a brief moment, she speaks into the receiver, her voice firm and confident. "Colonel, we've made a significant breakthrough. The Detective has identified the possible source and cure of the infection. I need to speak with you as soon as possible."

I can't help but wonder if this breakthrough is connected to the information I provided about the virus, or if it's about something else entirely. My uneasiness remains, but for now, all I can do is wait and see what unfolds.

Dr. Jennings continues, her voice steady and clear. "It seems that ArcticAde, the new soda that's been heavily marketed in our city, might be the source of the contagion. Furthermore, the Detective believes that blood types play a crucial role in the infection process, with AB+ blood type acting as a block or even a potential cure."

There's a brief pause as the Colonel responds, though I can't make out his words. Dr. Jennings listens intently, her expression a mixture of determination and concern. "Affirmative, sir. We need to delve deeper into this, but the data holds promise. It seems we might be onto a path that could terminate this nightmare." A gap of silence ensues as she takes in the Colonel's response. "Understood, sir." Her gaze lands on the soldier, "Sergeant, the Colonel requests a word with you." She hands the device over to him. As the soldier engages in conversation with the Colonel, his face takes on a serious demeanor, the kind that accompanies a direct order. The specifics of that command, however, elude me.

I start to notice that the numbness in my other hand is gradually beginning to fade as well. It seems that the progress I've made in regaining control over my body is spreading, and the sensation of triumph fills me. With each passing moment, I feel more and more determined to overcome this disease and regain my humanity. The hope that Dr. Jennings' breakthrough might lead to a cure only adds to my resolve.

While the soldier speaks to the Colonel, responding with a series of "Yes sir", "No sir", and "I understand, sir," Dr. Jennings busies herself with her notes. The atmosphere in the room is thick with tension as we all await the outcome of the conversation. The soldier's face remains stoic, betraying nothing of what the Colonel is telling him.

In an instant, the soldier hangs up the phone, his face expressionless as he marches purposefully towards Dr. Jennings. With a disturbingly practiced movement, he draws his pistol and presses the cold, unforgiving barrel to the back of her head. The deafening crack of the gunshot reverberates through the dimly lit room, a stark contrast to the sterile silence that once filled the space. Dr. Jennings' body crumples to the floor, her once-vibrant eyes now lifeless and staring into nothingness.

The soldier, determined to ensure Dr. Jennings' demise, fires several more rounds into her motionless body. Each shot punctuates the air with a brutal finality, leaving no doubt that the compassionate doctor will never awaken again. Grief washes over me for Dr. Jennings, whose pure intentions were met with a violent end.

My heart races as the soldier turns his cold, emotionless gaze towards me. As he approaches, my zombie nature reacts instinctively, causing me to growl at the soldier despite my desperate situation. I watch helplessly as he steps closer, the barrel of the gun unwaveringly focused on my forehead. In a futile attempt to protect myself, I instinctively raise the hand I can control in front of my face, bracing for the impending shots. Time seems to slow down as he pulls the trigger, and a searing pain explodes in my head, followed by a sudden darkness that clouds my vision.

In my semi-conscious state, I hear two additional shots ring out, each one echoing through the room, amplifying the sense of dread that has settled over me. I can feel warm blood pouring down my face, adding to the growing sense of despair. An endless silence follows, a suffocating void that feels as if death itself has taken hold.

9

I find myself confined within the cold, steel walls of a morgue freezer. Oddly, the interior feels like a crematorium, scorching hot and suffocating. The searing heat threatens to overwhelm me, and I want to scream, to call out for help, but my voice is silenced by the oppressive air.

As the pain becomes unbearable, my voice finally escapes my throat, but it emerges as a guttural zombie growl. I listen to myself in horror, realizing that the sound I'm making is nothing like my own voice. The growling continues, echoing within the confined space, but as the torment intensifies, the monstrous growls gradually transform into painful human screams, serving as a haunting echo of the agony I am experiencing.

Just as I feel like I can't bear it any longer, the freezer door swings open, revealing a concerned and familiar face. It's Sarah, her eyes filled with a mixture of worry and relief. She reaches out and pulls me from the hellish inferno, her touch a soothing balm against my scorched skin.

"Steve," she says softly, "dinner's ready."

The abrupt transition from the torturous heat to the comforting presence of Sarah leaves me disoriented, but I cling to her words like a lifeline, hoping they will anchor me back to the safety of reality.

As I catch my breath, the surreal nightmare takes a twisted turn. I find myself strapped to a morgue trolley, my limbs bound tightly by cold metal restraints. The sensation is akin to sleeping on my arm, the numbness enveloping my entire being. Yet, as if turning over in my sleep, the torpidity slowly dissipates, first from my arm, then from my legs and body.

The room around me is dimly lit, casting eerie shadows that dance along the walls as the flickering light reveals a grotesque gathering. Zombies, their rotting flesh and gnarled hands illuminated in the sinister half-light, crowd around the trolley with hungry eyes and guttural moans. Panic surges through me as the awful truth dawns on me: I am the dinner.

The zombies creep closer, their decaying faces contorted with ravenous anticipation. Their outstretched fingers, mere inches from my body, seem to reach for me in slow motion. My heart races, pounding against my chest as if trying to break free from its fleshy prison.

I try to scream, to break free from the restraints that hold me captive, but my voice is a mere whisper amid the overwhelming chorus of the undead's hungry groans. My vision begins to blur, the edges of the room fading into darkness as the horrifying scene threatens to consume me.

My eyes flutter open to see three flattened bullet casings, slick with blood, lying before me in a crimson pool on the table. I realize that they must have fallen out of my forehead when I turned my head to the side. In disbelief, I reach up to touch my forehead, feeling the impact points of the bullets. It seems my skull bone has evolved to become as strong as the arm shield that withstood the tank shell. I'm still in the laboratory, strapped to the table. Dr. Jennings' lifeless body lies on the floor, a tragic reminder of the chaos that has unfolded.

The room is bathed in a dim, red glow from emergency lights lining the walls. It seems that something significant has occurred since I slipped into semi-consciousness. Slowly, I become aware that I can move my entire body, the limitations of the virus and fever seemingly gone. Yet, it appears that my body has retained every evolutionary change it underwent during my time as a zombie.

I carefully examine my arm, discovering the spot where the bullet tore through when I instinctively tried to protect my face. To my amazement, the injury is nearly healed, revealing the shocking regenerative abilities my body now possesses. Similarly, the wounds on my forehead are also in the process of mending. It's clear that this harrowing experience has forever altered me, and now I must adapt to my new reality and capabilities in a world fraught with danger and uncertainty.

With newfound determination, I manage to unstrap myself from the table, yanking out the sedative feeding lines embedded in my arm in the process. I carefully swing my legs over the side, placing my feet on the cold floor. The feeling of control over my own body is both liberating and foreign, a stark contrast to the helpless state I'd been in due to the pathogen's influence. As I rise to my feet, I'm assailed by weakness and a gnawing hunger, as if I've been starved for days. Despite my shaky legs, I manage to stay upright, taking a few tentative steps forward.

Clad in my tattered and dirt-streaked detective suit, my first steps are shaky, my muscles protesting after being immobilized for an extended period. However, the more I move, the stronger I feel. As I take in my surroundings, my gaze falls on Dr. Jennings' lifeless body. A pang of sorrow and guilt hits me, as I remember how she tried to save me from this hellish nightmare, only to be ruthlessly executed by a soldier.

My heart feels heavy, knowing that she deserved better than this tragic end. I take a moment to pay my respects, silently thanking her for her selflessness and courage. With a determined resolve, I promise myself that I'll track down the colonel who ordered Dr. Jennings' execution and the sergeant responsible for carrying it out.

Crouching down beside her, I gently turn her over by grasping her hand in order to reach for the keycard hanging around her neck. Her skin feels cold to the touch, a stark contrast to the warmth she exuded in life. The moment my hand makes contact with her skin, something unexpected happens.

My hand transforms, taking on the appearance of Dr. Jennings' hand for a brief moment before reverting back to normal. I recoil in surprise, realizing that I seem to have gained the ability to absorb the DNA of those I willingly touch and morph my body parts accordingly. This newfound power leaves me both awestruck and wary of what it might mean for my future encounters.

I glance at the door, beyond which lies darkness, illuminated only by the faint glow of emergency lights. I know I must escape, leave this place behind, but I can't abandon Sarah and Mr. Washington.

They've been through just as much as I have, if not more. I have to find them and make sure they're both safe.

Inhaling deeply, I pick up the scent of Sarah. It's unmistakable and familiar, a beacon guiding me to her. Yet, deep within the recesses of my mind, something feels off about her scent. There's a nagging uncertainty, an uneasy sensation that I can't quite put my finger on.

Driven by a mixture of fear, hope, and determination, I step out into the dimly lit hallway. The underground complex stretches out before me, with debris and signs of struggle scattered throughout. I cautiously make my way through the maze-like corridors, listening intently for any signs of life or danger. The eerie silence is broken only by the distant hum of emergency generators, providing power to the bare minimum of systems needed to maintain the facility.

I advance slowly, peering into each room I pass. Most of them appear to be empty, showing signs of struggle—bullet holes riddle the walls in some places, while in others, blood stains and puddles hint at the violence that took place here. My surroundings accentuate the base's cold, functional aesthetic, designed with an unyielding focus on efficiency and security. As I traverse the corridor, I can't help but notice the signs pointing out that I'm currently nestled deep within sub-level 14 of this sprawling underground complex.

As I explore the level, I notice the corpses of soldiers and doctors, each with a single gunshot wound to the head. The termination of the base crew was thorough and merciless. I come across a small break room with vending machines, a microwave, and a coffee maker. Among the scattered items, I spot several ArcticAid bottles, realizing that many of the base crew were likely infected without their knowledge.

Knowing that I must find Sarah and escape, I realize I won't get far without energy. As much as time is of the essence, I need to take a moment to fill my belly. In the break room, I spot a burger and a bottle of cola on a plate, prepared recently but untouched. Cautiously, I place the burger in the microwave, staying alert for potential threats as I wait for it to heat up. The minute feels like an eternity as I keep my ears tuned to any sounds or signs of danger. Just before the microwave counts down to zero and rings to signal it's ready, I silently turn it off a second earlier, avoiding drawing unwanted attention.

With the burger now heated, I devour it like a man who hasn't eaten for days, the flavors bursting in my mouth with every bite. The burger is incredibly delicious—juicy meat, melted cheddar cheese, and a flavorful dressing create a symphony of taste. As I savor the meat, I can't help but wonder if my appetite for it is a lingering effect of my time as a zombie or simply a reminder that I'm a human omnivore. The juice from the burger runs down my chin, evidence of its succulence. Regardless, I've never eaten a burger like this before.

As I hold the bottle of cola in my hand, I carefully twist the cap, mindful of the noise it might make. The moment the seal breaks, a soft hissing sound escapes, as the carbonation is released. To me, in the silence that envelops the break room, the sound feels unnervingly loud—almost as if it's echoing off the walls. I freeze for a moment, acutely aware of my surroundings, my ears straining to detect any signs of danger that might have been alerted by the sound. After a few tense seconds, it seems that I'm still safe, and I proceed to drink the cola, enjoying the sweet, fizzy contrast to the savory meal I just consumed.

Even as I enjoy the meal, I can't shake the sense of urgency that has been gnawing at me. I know I must stay alert and be prepared for any potential threats. With every bite and sip, I listen carefully to my surroundings, ready to spring into action if necessary. This tension only serves to heighten my awareness and sharpen my senses, reminding me of the perilous situation I find myself in.

The scent of Sarah continues to lead me deeper into the base, past the holding cells, the communications center, and a small gym for the staff to maintain their physical fitness. Further along, I come across the storage room filled with emergency supplies. I notice that the weapons locker within the storage room has been emptied, a clear indication that there was an attempt to arm the base personnel. As I continue, I pass by other essential rooms that support the base's operation. Finally, I arrive at the main elevator shaft, a critical junction within the underground complex. I notice that the elevator is currently stationed at the top floor, indicating that whoever used it last must have gone up to the ground level.

In the dim, flickering light casting eerie shadows across the walls, I encounter a grisly scene. The soldier responsible for Dr. Jennings's death lies motionless on the cold concrete, a fireman's axe embedded deep in his skull. The scene narrates a grim story of a fierce struggle, evidenced by the weapon of choice ripped from its wall mount during the battle. The now-empty bracket, tarnished by scratches and smudges, is a mute witness to the frantic fight for survival. I can't shake off the thought that perhaps it was Mr. Washington who mounted this resistance against the sergeant, in a desperate attempt to escape this hellish ordeal.

Observing the ominous scene further, I notice the sergeant's pistol and ammunition conspicuously absent. Piecing together the clues, I deduce that Mr. Washington must have armed himself with these in his attempt to break free. If my assumption holds true, he is not just on the run; he is armed, dangerous, and resolute on surviving this ordeal.

With Mr. Washington's body nowhere in sight, it seems plausible that he was the one who left the base via the elevator, seeking an escape from this nightmare. As I take in the grisly scene, it occurs to me that the soldier must have made a fatal mistake during the confrontation, one that ultimately led to his own demise.

A mix of emotions churn within me. While I can't help but feel a pang of sympathy for the man who was just following orders, a stronger sense of justice washes over me. In some way, the soldier's fate feels like retribution for Dr. Jennings, who had her life brutally cut short due to her noble intentions.

I glance towards the source of Sarah's scent, which comes from deeper within the base, and then look back at the elevator. I take a deep breath, steeling my resolve as I reach down and carefully grip the handle of the fireman's axe embedded in the sergeant's skull. With a firm, determined tug, I wrench the weapon free, the sound of metal scraping against bone echoing through the dimly lit corridor.

Swiping Dr. Jennings' keycard, I call the elevator down to sub-level 14. The soft hum of machinery accompanies the descending elevator, a lone source of sound in the otherwise silent complex. When the elevator arrives, the doors slide open with a muted hiss.

As I peer inside the elevator, I'm met with another grim scene. A soldier's body lies sprawled on the floor, having been shot multiple times. The shots lack the precision one would expect from a trained soldier, which leads me to suspect that Mr. Washington was responsible for this as well during his escape. I feel a growing sense of admiration for the resilience Mr. Washington has demonstrated in his fight for survival, but it is tinged with sorrow at the cost of human life that continues to mount in this forsaken place.

In the dim, flickering light of the elevator, the soldier's lifeless eyes stare up at me, eerily mirroring my human form. A chilling reminder of the line that separates us, of life and death. I carefully step over the corpse to position myself inside the elevator. With a final, determined glance back towards the direction of Sarah's scent, I lodge the fireman's axe into the doorway, wedging it firmly to keep the doors from closing. This precaution will ensure that the elevator remains available, should Sarah and I need a swift exit.

I continue to follow her scent, my every step guided by the lingering aroma that leads me ever deeper into the underground complex. As I navigate the winding corridors, I pass by the lifeless bodies of soldiers and doctors, each one bearing the unmistakable signs of gunshot wounds.

My journey eventually brings me to a heavy security door, its imposing presence marked by a key card reader, a retinal scanner, and a fingerprint scanner. Two thick security windows, one on each side of the door, offer a glimpse into the decontamination chamber beyond it. Sarah's scent, stronger now than ever, wafts from the other side, confirming that she must be behind this door. My heart races as I ponder how to proceed, how to breach this seemingly impenetrable barrier.

Then, an idea strikes me. Dr. Jennings' keycard alone won't be enough, but perhaps, through some lingering connection to her, I can access the additional security measures. I concentrate, focusing my will on my hand and my eye, and, as if guided by some unseen force, my hand morphs into the shape of Dr. Jennings', and my eye adopts her retinal pattern.

With bated breath, I swipe the keycard, place my transformed hand on the fingerprint scanner, and gaze into the retinal scanner. To my amazement, the security system accepts the inputs and, with a heavy thunk, the door begins to unlock. As it slowly swings open, I steel myself for whatever may lie beyond.

Stepping through the now-open security door, I find myself in the empty decontamination chamber. The door behind me concludes its course with a definitive click, segregating the corridor I just left behind. An ambient luminescence pervades the room, casting an ethereal glow onto the sterilized surroundings.

A female computerized voice chimes in, guiding me through the disinfection procedure. "Please remain still while the decontamination process is underway," it instructs. I comply, standing motionless as an array of automated nozzles release a fine mist of disinfecting solution, enveloping me in a cloud of vapor that coats every inch of my body.

As the process comes to an end, the voice returns to inform me of the results. "Decontamination complete. No traces of contaminants detected. You are now clean." Relief washes over me, the confirmation that I am truly healed, despite my newfound abilities, providing a glimmer of hope in the midst of the unfolding chaos. Just as I begin to regain my bearings, the computer announces another update: "Ending lockdown."

Approaching the automatic door, it slides open, revealing only a pair of glowing yellow irises in the shadowy room beyond. These eyes seem to have been waiting patiently, like a predator anticipating its prey to stumble into its trap. Before I have a chance to react, a strong arm suddenly grabs my neck and hurls me through one of the thick security windows that lie near the door. Shards of broken glass surround me on the cold floor, glinting menacingly under the flickering lights.

The impact leaves me dazed and disoriented, but as my vision clears and becomes cleaner, I see the creature that attacked me climbing through the broken security window to come after me. It's then that I realize, with a harrowing sense of dread, that the attacker is none other than Sarah herself.

However, she is not the same person I remember. She has been horribly transformed, her body twisted and evolving into a creature beyond my wildest nightmares. I can see the virus has progressed rapidly, pushing her transformation to new heights. From the back of her body, an array of undulating tentacles and feelers have sprouted, encasing her in a nightmarish shell that vaguely recalls the form of a grotesque deep-sea creature. These tentacles move continuously, enveloping her as a parasitic fungus would its host.

Behind this monstrous veil, Sarah's terrified eyes are all that remain of her humanity. Buried within this horrific encasement, they stare out in fear and despair. She tries to speak, her voice muffled and distorted. "Help me!" she manages to gasp, the plea barely audible yet piercing in its intensity.

Preparing to move closer to help her break free from the horrifying encasement, the tendrils react. They lash out, seizing my limbs, and attempt to pull me towards Sarah's living prison. I fight against their constricting grasp, my newfound strength just managing to resist.

Touching the tendrils to free myself, I feel a powerful connection to the infection, as if it were a sentient entity. This bond links me to the infected neurons within Sarah, giving me access to the pathogen's own memories, as well as Sarah's experiences.

In a flash, I glimpse an advanced civilization that predated our own. This enigmatic society was far more advanced but fell victim to the disease, reducing the human population to mere thousands. It seems the contagion lay dormant for millennia beneath Arctic ice, biding its time.

The visions crystallize, revealing the infection's insidious puppetry through fever-induced dreams. I comprehend now that this virus is far more than a rudimentary pathogen; it's sentient, cunningly intelligent. Recognizing my resistance to assault others, it dismissed me as an inadequate host. It exploited my deepest emotions - my love for Sarah, my desperation to protect her - located her scent in the cobwebbed corners of my memories, and cunningly manipulated me into delivering the bite that could enable its transfer to a more compliant host, facilitating its continuous evolution. This explains the sudden shift of the undead horde on the bridge. After the bite, their focus wasn't Sarah. They sensed the virus's betrayal, its attempted exodus, and they wanted to eliminate the threat - me.

In a cruel twist, my resistance to its control transferred to Sarah when I bit her. This resistance forced the disease to adapt differently, growing outside Sarah's body instead of controlling her from within. As it enveloped her before being completely expelled, the pathogen created a monstrous cocoon that now encases her.

Having taken on the characteristics of a true parasite, the virus now seeks revenge on me, the host who caused it so much suffering. Its newfound sentience has given it a malicious intent— to kill me, the one who dared to defy its control.

Struggling against the insidious tendrils, my hand metamorphoses into claws once again. With swift and decisive strikes, I sever these parasitic appendages, only to realize that each inflicted pain on the creature is reflected in Sarah. Her anguished cries cut through the heavy silence, each one a dagger thrust into my heart, validating my worst fears—killing the parasite might also mean killing Sarah. Given the alarming rate at which the creature's appendages regenerate, I find myself faced with a reluctant conclusion: escape, not fight.

I dash through the shadow-laden corridors, my heart pounding as I try to widen the distance between myself and the parasitic creature. The dim, emergency lights cast fluctuating shadows on the walls, deepening the dread that permeates the air. As I hurtle down the narrow halls, the entity's menacing snarl and heavy footsteps relentlessly echo behind me, a terrifying reminder of its unwavering pursuit.

The smell of burnt electronics and the distant crackling of damaged wires fill my nostrils as I navigate the treacherous path ahead. I leap over overturned tables, debris, and other obstacles in my path, doing my best to maintain my speed despite the uneven terrain.

In stark contrast, the beast plows through everything in its way like a tank, seemingly unfazed by the devastation it leaves in its wake. The sound of shattering glass, splintering wood, and the groaning of twisted metal accompanies its rampage, serving as a chilling reminder of the creature's overwhelming strength.

Despite the terror that grips me, I can't help but be in awe of the sheer power and determination of the creature. With every labored breath and pounding step I take, I push my body to its limits, praying that I can somehow outrun the relentless horror that pursues me.

With renewed determination, I focus on reaching the elevator as my only means of escape. My legs propel me forward, taking me back to the familiar intersection I had encountered earlier. Skidding around the corner, I barely avoid colliding with the wall while changing directions. The instant I recover my balance, the monstrous creature barrels into the intersection right on my heels, mere moments away from capturing its prey.

The elevator looms ahead, its doors still open and beckoning me towards safety. The fireaxe I had wedged there earlier remains in place, its handle glistening under the dim emergency lights, proof of my foresight. Adrenaline courses through my veins as the distance between me and the elevator rapidly shrinks, the promise of escape within reach.

But just as I am about to cross the threshold, tendrils, sinewy and cold, coil around my neck, slamming me against the unforgiving concrete wall with brutal force. Their grip intensifies, each pulse of my heartbeat echoing in their tightening embrace. I can sense the perverse satisfaction of the virus through the tendrils' touch, a grotesque dance of death that intertwines with Sarah's tangible desperation. The sound of my neck bone cracking is unmistakable, yet the rapid healing process prevents it from shattering entirely.

Through the darkness of my encroaching doom, I witness the silent war in Sarah's eyes, a battlefield of will and despair as she wrestles against the monstrous parasite's control, a mirrored struggle of my own. Suddenly, the tendrils' unyielding stranglehold eases. Her voice cuts through the chaos, a desperate whisper carrying the weight of our shared torment, "Save yourself, you fool."

In a valiant act of defiance, Sarah's will wrests control away from the creature. Her eyes, filled with determination, lock onto mine, and she hurls me with staggering power into the elevator, an act of selfless sacrifice to save me. The impact against the cold, steel wall reverberates through my body, landing me amidst the lifeless remains of the soldier. The creature's roar of frustration echoes in the enclosed space, an anthem of its anger at losing control over Sarah, if only for a fleeting moment.

I kick the fire axe out of the elevator door, my hand slamming onto the control panel. The timeworn buttons protest under the exertion. Slowly, the doors start to shut, forging a formidable barrier between me and the beast. The creature lunges towards the narrowing gap, its colossal form crashing with a thunderous impact against the unyielding metal. The final sight I register is that of the enraged beast, its thwarted howls stifled by the robust metal barrier. Within this elevator, I find a transient sanctuary enclosed by steel walls, the creature held at bay - at least for now.

The elevator springs to life, carrying me away from the terror below. Its dim illumination throws eerie shadows, and the creature's distant roars echo hauntingly up the shaft. With every floor ascended, I feel a slight reprieve from the horror, even as an unsettling feeling lingers. As I near the top level, the self-healing process renews, mending my injuries.

The haunting image of Sarah's pain-wracked face and her desperate eyes, pleading for salvation, remains etched in my mind. I know I can't give up. I make a solemn vow to myself that I will do whatever it takes to save Sarah and put an end to this horrifying plague once and for all.

The doors open, revealing a large, abandoned lobby in utter disarray. Signs of struggle are evident everywhere—blood trails, bullet holes, and the lifeless bodies of soldiers, civilians, and doctors strewn across the floor. I glance at the windows, noticing that no daylight filters through the shattered panes, signaling that night has fallen outside.

As I make my way through the devastated lobby, I can hear the elevator doors close behind me, followed by the distinct hum of the machinery as it starts its descent. The realization hits me— the creature must have called the elevator back down, intending to follow me up to the ground floor.

I hastily exit the lobby, finding myself in the parking lot of what appears to be a large military base. However, upon closer inspection, it seems more like a disguised civilian research facility, nestled within the embrace of a dense forest and surrounded by imposing mountains. Recognizing one of the mountaintops in the distance, I realize that I might be somewhere northwest of the city.

The devastation is evident everywhere I look, telling a harrowing tale of a desperate struggle to contain the outbreak. Overturned, burning vehicles cast flickering shadows across the ground as plumes of smoke rise into the clear night sky, a canvas of twinkling stars bearing silent witness to the chaos below. It's clear that the military had purged the entire area, refusing to let anyone escape the building, in a ruthless effort to prevent the spread of the contagion.

As I stand in the parking lot, the scent of Sarah reaches my senses once again, growing stronger as the cocooned creature embracing her gets closer. Glancing back toward the lobby, I see that the elevator has started its return journey from Sub-Level 14.

Recalling Dr. Jennings' words, I remember that the infected body would either be consumed entirely by the pathogen within the next two to three days or resist it completely. I know she's still fighting, just like I did. If she resists the infection for three days, she might defeat it and return to normal.

A plan to save Sarah begins to form in my mind. I reach for the sniper rifle and several ammunition clips from one of the fallen soldiers; the cold metal feels reassuring in my grip. The sound of the bullet sliding into the chamber resonates as I load the weapon with practiced ease. From this point forward, I must walk a delicate line: acting as both her prey and protector, I must ensure her safety from zombies, soldiers, and even herself, while maintaining just enough distance to avoid becoming her prey myself.

Exiting the base, I follow the moonlit path that leads into the dense forest. As I disappear into the forest's shadowy folds, my heart pounds, priming me for the challenges that lie ahead. Her haunting growls and cries reverberate through the darkness as I delve deeper into the woods, serving as an ominous reminder that she's in relentless pursuit.

The most perilous game of cat and mouse has now commenced. Though the future is shrouded in uncertainty and the stakes have never been higher, one truth remains unshakeable: I won't abandon her – not now, not ever.

ACKNOWLEDGMENTS

I express my deepest gratitude to my family for their endless
patience when I would disappear into my writing haven,
often working late into the nights;
To my dear wife, Barbara,
And my beloved sons, Christopher and Blaise.

My heartfelt thanks go out to my diligent beta readers
for their invaluable feedback and dedication;
Emilie Magda,
Gloria McNeely,
Paula Esmo,
And Swords & Scythes Beta Reading,

And special thank you to my cover designer
for his patience and creativity;
Mirko Fermani

OTHER BOOKS BY STEPHEN WAYNE

Find all titles on Amazon:
amazon.com/stores/Stephen-Wayne/author/B0C8BB3Z8Y

THE LIGHTHOUSE OF FOOLS
A Science Fiction Novella

After losing everything, Thomas Harker retreats to the desert and begins building a lighthouse on barren land—an act seen as either madness or defiance. As the tower rises and the world takes notice, it becomes a symbol of hope, grief, and something far greater than anyone expected.

BIG LIES
A Science Fiction Thriller Novel

When astronomer Thomas Jeffries discovers an extinction-level asteroid, he's drawn into a secret world of elites plotting an off-world escape while keeping the public in the dark. As he uncovers ancient bloodlines, synthetic leaders, and engineered media, Jeffries must decide whether to join the chosen—or expose the truth to a world that may never see it coming.

THE LORD'S CANVAS
A Science Fantasy Novella

An ancient creator haunted by failure tries to rebuild the universe from a blank canvas, only to confront the shadows of his past. As old mistakes threaten to resurface, he must learn to listen, adapt, and collaborate— or risk repeating a cosmic tragedy.

FROM PEN TO PUBLISH
An Insider's Guide to Flawless Publication

This essential guide reveals the hidden challenges and critical steps of the writing journey, from first draft to publication. With practical strategies and candid insights, it empowers writers to turn their creative vision into lasting success.

COMING SOON

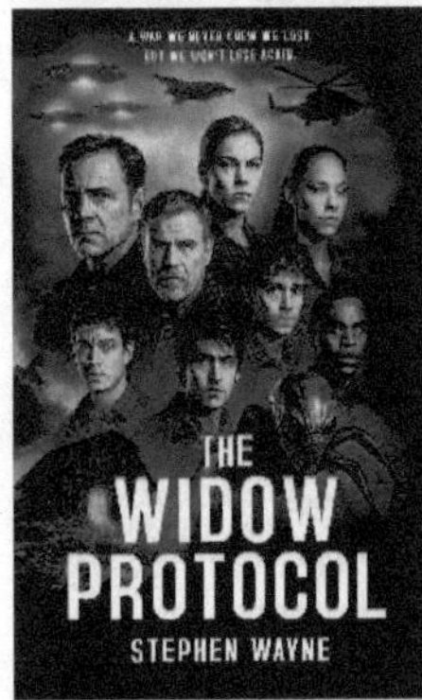

THEY DREAM IN COLOR
A Psychological Horror Novella

Exhausted and unraveling, new father John begins dreaming in vivid detail of alternate lives he never lived—until the dreams start reaching back. As the boundary between waking and dreaming breaks down, something from the other side threatens to take his place.

THE WIDOW PROTOCOL
A Science Fiction Horror Novel

When a prison bus breaks down in the Washington wilderness, a group of juvenile delinquents and their guardians uncover a hidden military base—and a war humanity already lost. To survive a shape-shifting enemy buried in silence and shadow, they must turn their troubled pasts into our last line of defense.

STEVE THE MONSTER
A Zombie Horror Novel

Sequel to Steve the Zombie.

ABOUT THE AUTHOR

Stephen Wayne is the pen name of István Szabó, a U.S. Horror Fiction bestseller and multi-award-winning author based in Hungary. He is also a professional book formatter and designer with an international client base spanning over 85 countries. His background includes work with law enforcement agencies on criminal investigations and with governmental agencies on national security matters.

In his downtime, Stephen is an avid adventurer whose pursuits span martial arts and extreme sports. He began training in Ju Jitsu at the age of ten and, for the past decade, has dedicated himself to kickboxing and Muay Thai. His interests also include long-distance running, fencing, and licensed scuba diving. A devoted father, he has dedicated himself to mastering all seven forms of lightsaber combat arts, sharing this modern discipline—a blend of traditional martial technique, cinematic choreography, and play—with his young son.

Stephen writes across multiple genres, including horror, science fiction, and philosophical fiction. Influenced by H.P. Lovecraft and Philip K. Dick, his work explores consciousness, identity, and the nature of existence through diverse stories—from cosmic horror and theological reimaginings to speculative futures and explorations of awareness itself.

Above all, he is a proud father to Christopher and Blaise, and a loving husband to Barbara.

CONNECT WITH THE AUTHOR

Official Author Website

www.waynebooks.com

Official Book Formatter Website

www.sapphireguardian.com

For translation rights, media adaptations,
or other permissions, contact:
stephen@waynebooks.com